THE
POCKET
WATCH
KILLER

M J EVANS

Book Publishing.com

Editing, design, typesetting and publishing by UK Book Publishing

www.ukbookpublishing.com

ISBN: 978-1-917329-96-5

THE
POCKET
WATCH
KILLER

CHAPTER ONE

———

"The Pocket Watch Killer Strikes Again" read the newspaper headline. This sent him into a rage. The killer lived in a static caravan on a caravan park in Cornwall. He was pacing up and down while he was reading the article. He put the newspaper down on the table and he went and sat on his bed. On the floor next to his bed was a box which he lifted up and put on the bed next to him. Inside the box were all different kinds of pocket watches. "Which one shall I use next?" he thought to himself. Now, he was getting ready to kill again.

As he was deciding which pocket watch to use, he heard the voice. Being a paranoid schizophrenic he heard the voice quite a lot. He was holding two watches, one in each hand. "Don't choose that one, choose the other one. You know, the one in your left hand," said the voice. He put the watch in his right hand back in the box.

For a little while he sat there looking at the watch. The more he looked at the watch the more he could hear the voice. The voice kept telling him that he needed to find another victim, he had to put right the wrong that had happened to him. Then, he stood up, put on his shoes and coat and went out.

In his right hand coat pocket was the pocket watch that he had chosen. He kept his hand in the pocket to make sure he didn't lose the watch. He didn't have any particular plan in mind, he just walked the streets until he found the right person.

After about two hours he spotted someone who he was interested in. The killer started to follow them. The person was a young woman in her early twenties. It appeared that the woman was heading towards the beach. It was a small, quiet beach where not many people visited and was away from the tourist areas. The woman descended the twelve or so steps that led from the public footpath down to the beach. She walked across the sand to the part of the beach where there were large rocks and boulders. When she got there, she sat down on one of the boulders and placed her bag next to her. This bag was a large canvas bag. Inside it she had a flask of tea, a bottle of water, a sandwich box filled with her favourite sandwiches, a book and a tartan blanket. With it being a really warm sunny day, she was planning on spending several hours on the beach.

Before she started to read her book she sat there for a little while to enjoy the sun and views. The killer was still on the footpath, watching her. He was leaning on the wall while he watched her. He was stood about three or four feet from the steps that the woman had gone down. As well as watching the woman, he was also surveying the area. The killer wanted to know what his escape routes were, how many people were in the area, if there were any police officers in the area and he was building himself up to do the deed.

While the killer was waiting for the best time to strike, Jordan was at home in Morecambe. Jordan Lewis is a private investigator and has just wrapped up another case. Jordan had been a police officer for fifteen years, but she didn't like the political side of the job. So, she took early retirement and became a private investigator. The case that she had just finished had been quite a difficult one and she was thinking about having a few days off. Jordan felt a little thirsty so she went to the kitchen to make herself a cup of tea. While she waited for the kettle to boil someone rang the doorbell. When she opened the front door Jarvis was stood there, so she let him in. Jordan had known Jarvis Moon for many years. Jarvis is a retired criminology professor and had taught Jordan for a couple of years when she first became a police officer and they had remained friends ever since.

"You always manage to turn up when I have the kettle on," said Jordan with a smile.

"I've always had good timing," said Jarvis.

"What are you doing here, anyway?"

"I may have a case for you, if you're interested," he said.

"I take it the case has something to do with that envelope you have in your hand?"

"Yes. This is from Carl Benson, an old professor friend of mine. When we have talked I have mentioned once or twice about you being a PI. When he retired a few years ago he moved down to Cornwall to live. Well, over the last couple of weeks there have been a couple of murders. Carl, being a criminology professor, has the feeling the police down there are struggling with this one. With that in mind he has sent me some information about the case and has asked me to show it to you. If you decided to take the case on, Carl will pay you your usual fees and expenses. If you agree, Carl said that he will book a couple of rooms in a bed and breakfast down there. Would that be okay?" he said.

"A couple of rooms, you say?"

"Yes, I've told him that I help you with a lot of your cases. Plus it would be nice to see an old friend again."

"I will be able to tell you more when I have read the information that he has sent you," she said.

At that, Jarvis handed over a large envelope. The two of them went into Jordan's office. Jordan sat at her desk and Jarvis sat in a comfortable chair next to the desk. Then, Jordan opened the envelope and spread the contents over her desk. The envelope was filled with newspaper articles and copies of police reports. It was obviously about the murders in Cornwall. The newspapers were reporting how a pocket watch had been left at the scene of the murders and the police couldn't understand how they were connected with the victims. When she had given the files and the articles a real good read Jordan sat back in her chair.

"This appears to be an interesting case, but I'm fascinated to know how Carl got hold of the police reports," said Jordan.

"Carl has a friend in the Cornwall police who asked him to have a look at the files, to see if he could offer any help. While he had them he took the opportunity to photocopy the files and sent them to me to show you on the off chance that you may be interested in working on the case," said Jarvis.

"Why does he want me to work on the case?"

"Because one of the victims is his granddaughter," said Jarvis.

"I was going to take a few days off after finishing my last case, but his seems an interesting case and Cornwall is a real nice part of the country. You can tell Carl that I will take on the case," said Jordan.

While the two of them were getting themselves ready to travel to Cornwall, the police down there received a phone call regarding another body being found. The body had been found on the beach where the killer had been watching the woman. When DS Mike Lucas arrived at the scene there was a small crowd beginning to gather. Once he was out of his car he looked over to the beach and he could see that Mandy Fletcher, the pathologist, was already with the body. As he was about to go over and have a look at the body, a car pulled up next to him. He saw that it was Jane Brown, part of the CSI team that worked the Cornwall area. Lucas waited for Jane and then the two of them approached the body together.

"Do you think this could be another one?" said Lucas.

"We will have to wait and see if we find a pocket watch," said Jane.

"I can't see the press here yet, but wouldn't you think that these people would have better things to do," said Lucas.

"Probably morbid curiosity," said Jane.

Soon, the two of them were stood next to the body. The first thing Jane did was to give the body the once over just in case there was any possible evidence. She didn't see anything *on* the body but there was something *near* the body. When she had a closer look she could see that it was a torn piece of material. Jane's first thought was that the victim had perhaps fought with the killer and she'd managed to tear off some of their clothing. She also knew that the piece of material could have nothing to do with the woman's death, but she had to take it in to evidence so that she could find out either way. When she had put the piece of cloth in an evidence bag, Jane, from where she was stood, looked around the crime scene to see what else she could spot. As she did so the sun came out from behind a cloud and she caught something glinting on a nearby rock. When she got to the rock she saw that it was a pocket watch. As soon as she saw what it was, she gave Lucas a shout.

"Have you found something?" said Lucas.

"Yeah, take a look at that," said Jane.

When he looked on the rock he saw the pocket watch. The two of them now knew that the victim, that was only a few feet away from them, was the work of the pocket watch killer.

Jordan and Jarvis had packed their bags and were about to begin their long journey down to Cornwall, totally unaware that there had been another body found. Jordan, in a way, was looking forward to arriving in Cornwall because it was one of her favourite parts of the country. With her not having visited there for a few years she had been considering having a holiday in Cornwall when she had finished the latest case anyway.

While Jordan was driving, Jarvis was reading the articles that Carl had sent to him. He was trying to understand the case. With him being a criminologist he was trying to work out how the killer was thinking. Jarvis was trying to find a pattern to these murders. Jarvis was also thinking about the relevance of the pocket watches. But at the moment, he had no idea what they meant.

Before he knew it they were very nearly at Cornwall and Jordan was pulling in to some motorway services. Jarvis was so engrossed with what he was doing he didn't realise they had travelled so far. While they were at the services they went to the toilet and got something to eat. When they had their food they found themselves a table to sit at. While they were eating they were talking about the case and what they could be facing when they arrived in Cornwall. When they had finished their meals and were just sat there talking, Jordan noticed someone sat at another table. To Jordan the person appeared to be glancing at them every so often.

"You see that guy over there, he appears to keep looking at us," said Jordan.

"You're being paranoid. We're not even in Cornwall yet and you think we are being followed," said Jarvis.

"I'm not being paranoid; he does keep looking at us. On top of that I seem to recognise him from somewhere."

At that point, someone dropped something – their tray with their drinks and glasses on – which caught their attention. And when Jordan looked back the person that she had noticed had now gone. So, the two of them went back to Jordan's car to finish the rest of the journey to Cornwall.

Meanwhile, back at the beach, Mandy Fletcher, the pathologist, was still examining the body; Jane Brown, the CSI, was still searching for any possible evidence and

Lucas was looking around the crime scene trying to work out what had happened. Unknown to any of them the killer was in the small crowd watching what they were doing. Lucas, for some reason, stopped what he was doing and started to look at the crowd. As he was looking at the crowd he thought he saw someone he knew, but he couldn't think where from. For a minute or two he didn't think much of it, but then he realised it was someone that he had arrested before. So, he went to have a talk with him. As Lucas approached this person, for one brief moment, it looked to the killer who was watching them like he was walking towards him. This unnerved the killer and he started to walk away. As he did so, he looked towards Lucas and saw that he was talking to someone else. The killer gave a huge sigh of relief and carried on walking.

The killer then started to make his way back to the caravan park where he lived. For now, the voice that he kept hearing was silent. With the voice being silent the need to kill had subsided. On his way home he passed a café and he decided to go in for a coffee. With it being a nice day he decided to drink his coffee sat at one of the small outside tables. While he was drinking his coffee he noticed Professor Carl Benson, Jarvis's friend, sat in his car outside a bed and breakfast. The killer knew Carl quite well because Carl had taught him at university for a little while. Even though the killer is a schizophrenic it wasn't always out of control as it is now. When the killer was at university he was taking his medication, which helped to keep his condition under control and he was able to lead quite a normal life. But when he came off his medication, as it gave him terrible headaches, that was when it all changed.

While he was sat there drinking his coffee, he noticed another car pull up and a man and a woman got out of the car. The man and the woman were Jordan and Jarvis. "I will have to find out who that is," the killer thought to himself.

When Carl saw who had arrived, he got out of his car and went across to them. He shook hands with Jarvis who, in turn, introduced Jordan. The three of them spoke for a moment or so, then, Jordan and Jarvis got their bags out of the car and the three of them went into the bed and breakfast. The owner of the bed and breakfast gave them the keys to their rooms and they made their way upstairs with the owner leading the way. When the owner had showed them to their rooms she went back downstairs. When they got to their rooms the three of them went into Jordan's so they could talk in private about the case.

"Have you read the information that I had sent to Jarvis?" Carl asked Jordan.

"Yes, I did," said Jordan.

"So, what do you think?" said Carl.

"I think that it looks like a challenging case and I can't wait to get started," said Jordan.

"Good, I'm so pleased that you've decided to take the case. All I need to know is how much you charge?" said Carl.

"My fees are £2,500 a week plus expenses with the first £500 up front," said Jordan.

"Would you like the £500 in cash?" said Carl.

"If that would be okay," said Jordan.

Carl counted out the money and gave it to her. What Jordan wanted to do now was to go out for a little while and get a feel for the area. While she did that, Jarvis went to his room, which was right next door, to unpack, and Carl went with him. It was almost a quarter to four in the afternoon but it was still sunny and warm. When she came out of the bed and breakfast, Jordan stood there for a moment to decide which direction to go. When she looked at some nearby road signs she could see that one of them said "To the Beach", so she decided to go in that direction. Jordan was totally unaware that the killer was still sat outside the café and was watching her. As Jordan started to walk towards the beach, the killer stood up and started to follow her.

As the beach came into view, Jordan could see a small crowd that were watching something on the beach. So, she went across to have a look at what was happening. As she got a little closer she saw a van with Scientific Unit on the side and a black van parked near the beach. When Jordan was in position to look, on the beach she saw the pathologist dealing with a dead body, a CSI dealing with what appeared to be some evidence, and she also saw Lucas with Jane the CSI. Jordan's experience told her that Lucas was a police officer who was in charge of the crime scene. While she was stood there watching, Jane, the CSI, started to walk in the direction of Jordan and she had a clear plastic evidence bag in her hand. When Jane was close enough Jordan could see that it was a pocket watch inside the evidence bag. Jordan took her notebook and pen out of her jacket pocket and started to make notes. With a pocket watch being taken into evidence, Jordan knew that this crime scene had to have something to do with the case that Carl had asked her to look into. As Jordan was taking notes, Lucas noticed her. At first, he thought she was a reporter so he went to have a chat with her. As Lucas walked across the beach, Mandy, the pathologist, called over to him. When Lucas reached her, Mandy told him that she was taking the body back to the morgue. When he looked towards where Jordan was stood, she wasn't there any more.

Now that she had come across another potential murder committed by the pocket watch killer, Jordan wanted to inform Carl about it straight away. She just wished she had her camera with her. Jordan likes taking photos when she is working a case because having something visual to look at helps her to piece the case together which in turn helps her to solve the case. Soon, she was back at the bed and breakfast and making her way to Jarvis's room. As Jordan approached Jarvis's room, the door opened and Carl came walking out and Jarvis stood at the door. When they saw Jordan, the two of them went back into the room. Jordan followed them in and closed the door.

"I think I've stumbled onto another murder committed by the pocket watch killer," said Jordan.

"What makes you say that?" said Jarvis.

"While I was walking round getting a feel for the area, I found my way to the beach which isn't too far away from here. There was a small crowd of people watching something on the sand, so I went to see what it was. When I got to where the crowd was I could see a pathologist dealing with a body, a CSI looking for evidence and a police officer giving the scene a once over. The CSI had an evidence bag in her hand. When I was able to have a good look at what was in the evidence bag, I could see that it was a pocket watch. Because of that watch I knew that the pocket watch killer was responsible for the victim's death," said Jordan.

Now, the three of them knew that the pocket watch killer had struck again. They knew it was as important as ever to find the killer and put him in prison, where he belongs.

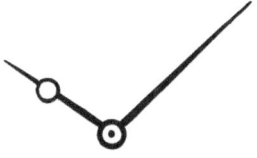

CHAPTER TWO

It was almost ten o'clock at night and Jordan was in her room in the bed and breakfast. She was looking through what Carl had sent to Jarvis and thinking about what she had seen on the beach earlier that afternoon. Then, mainly because of the long journey, Jordan began to feel really tired. As she was about to get ready for bed, she shivered slightly. When she looked across to the window she realised the window was still open, so she went across to close it. She was just about to close the curtains when she noticed someone stood outside. Jordan's room was on the side of the building which overlooked the side street. The person was wearing dark coloured training shoes, black jogging trousers and a black hooded sweatshirt with the hood over their head. The person was stood across the street, smoking a cigarette and appeared to keep glancing up at Jordan's window.

Jordan pretended not to notice the person and closed the curtains. She knew that it could be nothing, but she was really curious about it and was wondering if this individual was involved with the case somehow. So, even though she was really tired, she knew she had to check it out. Jordan knew Jarvis was probably asleep, so she left the room and closed the door as quietly as she could in an attempt not to disturb him. As she was making her way out of the bed and breakfast, Jordan saw Hazel Davis, the owner of the bed and breakfast.

"Don't forget I lock up at eleven," said Hazel.

"I will be back before then," said Jordan.

When she left the bed and breakfast, Jordan went straight for the street the person was on. The street was on the left hand side of the bed and breakfast. When she got to the street and looked down she could see the person still standing there; Jordan wanted to know who the person was and if they had anything to do with the case. When she started to make her way down the street the person saw her and began to walk away. Straight away this made Jordan suspicious. Jordan tried her best to catch up with the person but the quicker she went the quicker they went. As Jordan was beginning to catch them up, the person, very quickly, went down an alley. When Jordan got to the end of the alley she could see there were no lights down the alley and it was very dark. Nevertheless, Jordan was sure she could see some movement.

As Jordan was stood wondering whether to follow or not, a light came on and she saw the person that she was following. At this point, the two of them looked at each other. Then, the stranger set off running and Jordan set off after them. When she was part way down the alley the light went off, then, when she went a little further the light came back on. This told Jordan the light was attached to a motion sensor. When Jordan reached the end of the alley she couldn't see the stranger anywhere. But where she was stood she could see the part of the beach where the dead body was found earlier. Near where she was stood there was a row of shops and cafes which were closed. On the off chance the stranger was hiding, Jordan went for a walk up and down the main road. After a few minutes of looking around and with no sign of the stranger, Jordan decided to go back to the bed and breakfast.

As Jordan made her way back there, she was totally unaware that the stranger was still nearby. The stranger was hiding on the beach where the most recent body was found. From where he was he could see Jordan about to head back down the alley. As he was about to move from his hiding place he saw someone follow Jordan down the alley. The stranger wasn't sure where exactly this other person came from, but he was curious to know why they were following Jordan. So, out of curiosity the stranger went to see what the other person was up to. When the stranger got to the end of the alley Jordan was about to walk past the light with the sensor. When the light came on the stranger saw that the other person was about to grab Jordan.

"Hey," shouted the stranger.

At this point, the person who was about to grab Jordan ran off past her and then the stranger went in a different direction. Jordan just stood there wondering what was happening. She was sure the one at the end of the alley, the one that had shouted, was the stranger that she had followed. But the other one had got her thinking. Then, it dawned on her. She started to think that, just perhaps, the other one might be the killer. With the killer possibly still being nearby, Jordan made her way back to the bed and breakfast as quickly as she could.

When she got back to the bed and breakfast it was almost twenty-five to eleven. She went straight in and up to her room, then sat on her bed. Jordan sat there and thought about what had happened in the last half an hour or so. She was as sure as she could be that the person in the alley, the one that was going to grab her, was the killer. But she was curious to know why the first stranger, the one she had followed, had scared the other one away. While she was thinking about this she slowly started to get herself ready for bed. The one thing she was thinking so hard about was what the two strangers' faces looked like, but for the life of her she just didn't know. For the first stranger, he was wearing a hooded sweatshirt with the hood over his head and she never got a good look at his face. The second stranger from the alley, all she got was a good look at the back of his head as he ran away. Before she knew it she was drifting off to sleep.

All too soon, it was the following morning and Lucas was arriving at the station. When he reached his desk he saw that someone had put the morning newspaper on his desk. When he picked up the paper he saw the headline said, "The Third Pocket Watch Killing". Lucas just sighed as he sat in his seat. When he turned on his computer he saw that he had an email from Mandy, the pathologist, sending him her autopsy report. When he looked at the section that gave the cause of death he could see that it said just one word: garrotted. This was the same cause of death for the first two victims of the pocket watch killer.

Back at the bed and breakfast, Jordan was beginning to wake up. When she was out of bed she had her usual morning shower and got dressed. All the time she was thinking about what had happened the previous night. Once she was dressed she made her way downstairs for breakfast, first making sure that she had her room key. When she was in the hallway she went to the room next door to see if Jarvis was ready for breakfast. Within a few seconds of her knocking, the door opened and Jarvis was stood there.

"Are you ready for breakfast?" said Jordan.

"Yes, I'm so hungry I could eat a horse."

"You're always that hungry."

When Jarvis had come out of his room and closed the door, the two of them made their way to the dining room. As they did so a door to one of the other rooms opened slightly and the occupant watched them walk away. When the two of them walked into the dining room they could see it was a large room with eight tables for guests to have their breakfasts. When Hazel, the bed and breakfast owner, saw them she came across and showed them to a table.

"Would you like tea or coffee?" said Hazel.

"Could we have tea for two," said Jordan.

Hazel went back to the kitchen to get them their drinks.

"So, where did you go to last night?" said Jarvis.

"How do you mean?" said Jordan.

"I heard you leave your room about ten o'clock, then, I heard you come back about half an hour later."

"Well, I was getting myself ready for bed when I glanced out of the window. As I looked out of the window I saw someone standing outside having a smoke. As I was watching him he appeared to keep looking up at my window. So, I went to have a chat with him."

"What did he have to say for himself?"

"Not a lot. When he saw me heading towards him he started to walk away. I followed him and I tried my best to catch up with him, but I lost him. I looked around for him for a little while, but I couldn't find him. Then, I came back here and went to bed," said Jordan.

Jordan decided not to tell Jarvis about the second stranger, the one that almost grabbed her, because she didn't want to worry him. Just then, Hazel came back to their table with a teapot and cups, followed very soon after with their breakfasts.

While the two of them ate their breakfasts, the killer was at his home on the caravan park. He was relaxing in his armchair drinking a cup of coffee and watching TV. As he was sat there he heard what appeared to be a number of cars pulling up. When he looked out of the window he saw that it was a couple of police cars. As he was stood there watching he saw four officers, two from each car, open the car doors and get out. The four of them stood at the front of one of the cars and started to talk. All the while the killer was wondering why they had come to the caravan park. After the officers had been there for about ten minutes one of the officers walked to the killer's static caravan and knocked on the door. At this point, the killer became really unnerved; then, when the killer thought for a moment or two the killer knew there was no way out of it and he had to open the door. He went to the door, slowly opened it and peered out.

"Hello there, sorry to disturb you but would it be ok if I used your toilet?" said the officer.

The killer gave a sigh of relief and said, "Of course you can."

The killer stood to one side and let the officer in. When the officer was in the killer closed the door and showed the officer where the bathroom was. All the while the officer was in his home, he was becoming more and more anxious. Then, he heard the voice. "He knows you can't let him leave." Then, he could hear the toilet flush and he saw the officer walking towards him. It took a lot of strength to ignore the voice, he couldn't risk any complications.

"Thanks for that, I really needed that," said the officer.

"That's okay," said the killer.

"Have we ever met before?" said the officer.

"No, I don't think so," said the killer.

"I'm sure we've met before because you look so familiar. Well, thanks again," said the officer.

At that, the officer opened the door and walked out. When he was outside all the officers got back into their cars and drove out of the caravan park. The killer gave a large sigh of relief.

Back at the bed and breakfast Jordan and Jarvis were just finishing up their breakfast. At the same time, Carl, Jarvis's friend, was just arriving at the bed and breakfast. He saw them in the dining room, so he joined them at their table.

"Good morning," he said.

"Good morning," they replied.

"Would you like a cup of tea?" said Jordan.

"No, I'm fine, thank you. I was wondering, when you have finished your breakfasts, if the two of you would like to go and look at the first two crime scenes?" said Carl.

"We would love to," said Jordan.

The two of them finished their breakfasts, then, they followed Carl out to his car. Jarvis sat in the front with Carl and Jordan sat in the back. While they were travelling Jordan was looking out of the car window. She could hear Jarvis and Carl talking but she wasn't paying much attention. Every person they passed Jordan looked at them as closely as possible. She was trying to see if she could find the two people from the previous night. The next thing she was aware of the car was slowing down to a stop. When Jordan looked she could see they were stopped at a set of traffic lights. While they waited for the lights to change back to green Jordan glanced out of the front windscreen. As she did so she noticed someone crossing the road. When she looked more closely she was sure that the person crossing the road was the first stranger that she had seen the night before.

Without saying a word, Jordan got out of the car to have a chat with this person. But in getting out of the car Jordan had, for a moment, lost the person in the crowd. Then, she spotted them a little way in the distance and she set off after them. Despite going as quickly as she could, Jordan didn't seem to be catching them. Then, the person went down what appeared to be a side street and when Jordan reached the end of the street she couldn't see the person anywhere. Knowing the person could have spotted her following them Jordan very slowly started to walk down the street. She was looking everywhere, because the person could be anywhere.

She knew the person was somewhere on the street, but she didn't know exactly where. Then, she realised that they could be in one of the houses.

When she was a little way down the street she heard a house door open and close behind her. When she turned round she saw someone walking down the path to one of the houses. When she had a closer look she was sure this was the person that she had seen from the car, but now she wasn't sure if they were actually the same person as the previous night. As this person got to their gate Jordan saw that it was a young woman and she saw Jordan looking at her.

"Can I help you?" said the woman.

"No, thank you. I think I've mistaken you for someone else," said Jordan.

The young woman smiled and went on her way. Unbeknown to Jordan she was being watched from a short distance away. The person that she had been following was the person from the previous night, the one that she had seen from her room, and they had noticed Jordan following them. The stranger did live on the street and were watching Jordan from their bedroom window.

While Jordan was following the stranger, Carl and Jarvis were driving round the streets trying to find her. Then, they turned down the street that Jordan was on and they spotted her. Jordan saw them pull up, so, she decided to give up looking for the stranger and got into the car. She explained why she'd rushed off. Then Carl drove off to show them the first crime scene as planned. The stranger smiled as they drove off and continued with what they were doing.

Meanwhile, Lucas was still sat at his desk. He was wondering to himself if they would catch the pocket watch killer. They don't know what the killer looks like, they didn't have any witnesses and they don't have any evidence, except for the pocket watches, that could point them in the right direction. Even with the pocket watches, nobody knew their relevance to the case, if anything. While he was sat there in a little world of his own he received an email. He snapped himself out of his daydream and clicked on to the email. When he opened the email he saw that it contained photos of the three crime scenes. Assuming they came from the crime lab, Lucas started to look through them. As he was looking through the photos he thought there was something a little odd about them, but he couldn't quite put his finger on what it was. At this point, he began to look at each photo more closely. After a minute or two it dawned on him: only the dead body was in the photos. If these were police photos they would have more people in them like himself, Mandy the pathologist, Jane the CSI and some of the photos would have members of the public who had stopped to watch them. There wasn't even any crime scene tape up to protect the scene. This told him that only one person could have sent him the email and that was the killer. When he got to the last photo there was a short message at the end of the email. The message said, "What do you think of my handiwork?"

Straight away Lucas was curious about a couple of things. Firstly, if the email was from the killer, for which Lucas had no doubt, how did he gain access to Lucas's email address, and secondly, where did the killer send the email from? To get the sender's address, he went back to the top of the email. He could see that it was sent from the local library. Lucas wrote down the relevant information for the email, then, he went to the library to see if they had any information about the person who had sent it.

Soon, Lucas was in his car making his way to the library. While he was driving he was wondering if the person who sent the email was still in the library. Before he knew it he was at the library and parking his car. This particular library was on two levels. The ground floor level had the enquiry desk, children's books, fiction books, non-fiction books and so on. Upstairs had the reference section and the computers. Lucas went straight to the enquiry desk. When he got to the desk there was a young woman standing there. The young woman was in her late teens to early twenties, she wore black boots, black jeans, black T-shirt, her hair was black, both of her ears were pierced and she had a tattoo of a wolf on her upper left arm. The first thought Lucas had was the young lady had to be a Goth. With the name tag on her T-shirt he could see that her name was Carla.

"Hi Carla, I'm DS Mike Lucas from the local police and I was wondering if you could help me," he said as he showed his police identification.

"If I can," said Carla.

"I received an email about half an hour ago from someone using a computer in this library. I was wondering if you could tell me if they are still logged on," said Lucas.

"If I had their user name I could check on my computer here," said Carla.

At that, Lucas handed over to Carla all the user information that he got from the email and she went on the computer that was in front of her.

"According to this, Pocket Watch, Pocket Watch being the user name, is still logged on," said Carla.

"Could you show which computer it is?" said Lucas.

At that, the two of them made their way upstairs to the computers. When they were at the right computer they could see that it was still logged on and in use, but no one was sat in front of it. The member of staff who looked after the computers saw them stood there and went over to them.

"The one using this computer, do you know where are?" said Carla.

"Yeah, he's just going downstairs," he said.

Just then, the person going downstairs glanced over to them. He saw them looking at him and then he set off running out of the library. At that point, Lucas took up the chase. As Lucas got to the bottom of the stairs he saw the person running out of the door. The person that Lucas was following headed around the library to where Lucas had parked his car. But when Lucas had got round to that side of the building he couldn't see the person he was chasing anywhere, it was as if he had vanished into thin air. Lucas knew that there was every chance that the person he was chasing was the pocket watch killer and that he couldn't be too far away. For the next several minutes Lucas walked up and down the street looking for the person he was chasing. When he couldn't see the person anywhere Lucas knew that they had got away.

Before he went back to the station Lucas returned to the library to see if this individual he had just chased had left anything behind. He was totally unaware that while he was walking back to the library he was being watched by the person he had just been chasing. Quite near to the library was a small block of public toilets and the person was hiding behind them. This person was the killer and when he saw Lucas go into the library he came out of his hiding place and went home.

When Lucas was in the library he went straight upstairs to where the computers were. He could see that Carla was stood next to the computer that the killer had been using. Carla asked him what he wanted her to do with the computer. Lucas told her to leave everything as it was because he would be getting someone from the crime lab to check it out. Soon, Jane, the CSI, was arriving at the library. Jane used the library frequently so she knew where the computer section was and she went straight up. Upstairs, she saw Lucas standing next to one computer so she went across to join him.

"I take it that this is the computer that you want me to have a look at?" said Jane.

"Yeah, I will be interested in the fingerprints that you get off it. Also, there are a pen and a notebook that need to go into evidence," said Lucas.

Jane put the pen and notebook into separate evidence bags and she would give them a closer look back at the lab. Then she pulled out of her bag a jar of fingerprint powder and a special brush for dusting for fingerprints. She then dusted the computer, the keyboard and the table the computer was on. When she had finished checking for fingerprints she had one last look to make sure she hadn't missed anything. When Jane was happy that she hadn't missed anything she packed away everything, including the evidence, back into her case and then she went back to the lab. At this point, Lucas told Carla that they could use the computer again and he returned to the station, still kicking himself that he hadn't managed to catch the individual that he had chased earlier.

CHAPTER THREE

———

While the killer was making his way home the voice started to talk to him again.

"You need another one," said the voice.

He tried and tried to ignore the voice, but he couldn't. It kept on saying over and over that he needed another and it wouldn't stop. Soon, he was home. When he was inside and the door was closed, he started to pace up and down.

"Don't forget to choose a watch," said the voice.

He went over to the box of pocket watches that he had, picked them up and sat on his bed. For a moment or two he just sat there looking at the watches.

"Go on, choose one. You know you have to," said the voice.

The killer selected a couple of watches and put the box with the rest in on the floor. While the killer contemplated which watch from the two he was holding to use, he decided to lie down on his bed.

While he lay there he started to feel tired. Before he knew it he was fast asleep. No sooner was he asleep then he started to dream. The dream started with him being in a hospital. It wasn't a general hospital he was in, it was a psychiatric hospital. In the dream he was wearing a white gown and was walking along a very long corridor. It appeared that he was the only one in the hospital as he couldn't see or hear anyone else. While he was walking he saw a door at the end of the corridor, so he walked towards it. When he got to the door and opened it, he found himself in an operating room. In the middle of the operating room there was an operating table with what appeared to be hospital staff stood around it; other than that the room was completely empty. The people he saw were dressed in hospital gowns that are used by surgeons and their staff. When he had walked over to them, he saw that it was him that they were about to operate on. He saw that his head had been shaved and as the surgeon was about to make his first cut with his scalpel, the killer turned away and started to walk towards the door. When he reached the door and opened it, he found himself outside. As he looked around he saw that he was in a cemetery, but he could only see three graves. So, he walked across to have a look at them. He read the headstones but all they said was Jane Doe and their date of death. He then realised that these were the graves of his three victims. While he was stood there another grave opening appeared. As he looked across he saw the gravedigger standing there and he was leaning against his shovel. The gravedigger was in his late fifties to early sixties, and was wearing work boots, trousers, a shirt, a flat cap and was smoking a pipe. The gravedigger took the pipe out of his mouth, smiled and said, "Don't forget the pocket watch."

At that, the killer bolted awake. He sat on the edge of the bed and thought about what he had just dreamt about for a moment or two. Then, he looked at the two pocket watches that he had chosen from the box and tried to decide which one he would use. Once the decision was made, he put on his shoes and coat, put the watch in his coat pocket and went out.

While he was walking the streets looking for another victim, the killer couldn't hear the voice and he didn't have the urge to claim another victim. But instead of going back home he continued to walk around so he could get some fresh air. And while he was walking an idea came to him. What he wanted to do was to lay down a challenge to the police, so he made his way to the police station. For a few minutes he stood outside, building up the nerve to go in. While he was stood there he could see people coming and going from the station, some were police officers and some were members of the public. When there were five or six members of the public in the reception area, he decided to go into the station. The reception area was quite large. Along one side, opposite the door, was a long desk with a large perspex glass. The perspex glass was there to protect the officers from anyone trying to attack them. On the right hand wall there was a door. This allowed members of staff to go behind the desk or other parts of the station. On the same wall as the door was a noticeboard filled with information for the public to read. Under the noticeboard there was a row of seats. The killer went and sat on one of those seats.

While the killer sat there, Lucas came down to reception to speak with someone. The killer had seen Lucas at the third crime scene and recognised him straight away. At this point, the killer put the watch that he had brought with him on the chair next to him and then walked out of the station. When Lucas had finished with the person he was talking to he glanced over to the chairs and saw what the killer had left. When he walked across and saw that it was a pocket watch he knew the killer had been in the station. At this point, he took a handkerchief out of his trouser pocket and picked up the pocket watch. He used the handkerchief so he wouldn't disturb any possible fingerprints that the killer had left on the watch. When he was back upstairs and had put the pocket watch on his desk he gave Jane, the CSI, a call. When Lucas had told Jane what he had found in the reception area of the station, she made her way there as quickly as she could.

At the same time, Carl, along with Jordan and Jarvis, were arriving at the scene of the first murder. The scene was on another beach and was just inside the opening to a cave. It appeared to be a very quiet and secluded place. Even now on a bright sunny day the three of them were the only ones on this particular beach. For several minutes Jordan walked through the scene in silence. She was trying to get a picture in her mind of exactly what had happened. She did something like this on every case because it really helped her to solve the case.

While the three of them were on the beach they could see someone coming on to the beach at the far end. When they saw that this person had a dog with them they thought it likely just someone making the most of a nice day and so they didn't think anything else of it. What they didn't know was that the one walking the dog was David Crammer, an ex-con who was really interested in the case. David lived on the same caravan park as the killer but didn't realise it. As he got on to the beach he let his dog off the lead, so she could run around. David and his dog were heading in the general direction of that cave where Jordan, Jarvis and Carl were looking around. When he was close enough to have a better look at them, David recognised Jordan. A few months earlier a case that Jordan had solved was in all the national newspapers along with a photo of Jordan. Because of the photo, David was able to recognise her and it led him to think that Jordan was now working on the case of the pocket watch killer.

As David got closer to the cave, Jordan decided that she had seen enough and she wanted to go to the second crime scene. So, the three of them started to make their way back to Carl's car. As they were walking away from the cave, Jordan had a quick glance at the person walking their dog, then, she looked away again. For some reason Jordan seemed to know him from somewhere but she couldn't put her finger on where from.

When they were in the car travelling to the second crime scene, Jordan began to wonder if the dog walker she had just seen was the one she had followed the previous night, the one she saw through the window. The second crime scene was at a cemetery. It was a large cemetery; it was so large, in fact, Carl could drive around it. Carl stopped the car at an area of the cemetery where there were no graves. There was still some crime scene tape visible from where the police had cordoned off the crime scene. Jordan, Jarvis and Carl got out of the car. As with the first crime scene, Jordan started to have a little look around, to try to give her a feel for the crime and help to get into the mind of the criminal.

While Jordan was walking round the second crime scene something caught her eye. When she went across to see what it was, she saw that it was a wallet. Jordan didn't want to put her own fingerprints on the wallet, so, she checked her pockets to see if she had a handkerchief. When she found one in her jacket pocket, she bent down and picked up the wallet using the handkerchief as she did so. Jarvis and Carl walked over to see what she had found.

"You've found something, then," said Jarvis.

"Yeah, I've found someone's wallet, but I don't know if it has anything to do with the case," said Jordan.

"Is there any identification inside?" said Jarvis.

When Jordan opened the wallet she found a driving licence. When she looked at the photo on the licence she saw that it was the dog walker that she had seen on the beach earlier. Now, because of the driving licence, Jordan had this person's name and address. She knew that she had to hand the wallet over to the police and tell them where she had found it, but not before she went to talk to David Crammer, the owner of the wallet.

Meanwhile, David Crammer had finished walking his dog and was making his way home, with his dog walking beside him. David knew he had lost his wallet but had no idea where. As David made his way home, Jordan, Jarvis and Carl were making their way there too. Finding David's wallet was, at the moment, Jordan's best lead on the case and she was going to use it to her advantage.

Soon, the three of them were arriving at the address where David lived. Straight away they saw that it was a caravan park with the vast majority of them being static caravans, with some people making them their homes. As they were driving around trying to find the static caravan where David lived, the killer was just arriving home. As he unlocked and opened the door, Carl stopped just in front of David's caravan, which was opposite the killer's. When he saw the three of them start getting out of the car the killer hurried into his caravan and closed the door. Once inside, he started to watch them through the window. The killer had an uncomfortable feeling that they were looking into the murders that he had committed, but he was curious to know why they were going to David's caravan.

When the three of them were out of the car Jordan knocked on the door of David's static caravan. When there was no answer after a minute or so, Jordan knocked on the door for a second time. But while they were stood there waiting for an answer, Jordan saw someone walking towards them with a dog. When he got a little closer to them Jordan realised that it was David Crammer, the owner of the wallet and the one she had seen walking on the beach earlier.

"Didn't I see the three of you on the beach a little while ago?" said David as he reached them.

"Yes, you did," said Jordan.

"Then, why are you here?" said David.

"Well, I'm Jordan Lewis, a private investigator and I've been employed to look into the recent murders in the area. The reason why we are here is because we have found some evidence that led us here," said Jordan as she showed her ID.

"Yeah and what evidence is that?" said David.

"We found your wallet at the second crime scene," said Jordan.

At that, David stopped and went quiet. He was obviously thinking about what Jordan had just said. After a moment or so David unlocked and opened the door to his static caravan. Then, he invited the three of them inside. While they were making their way inside the killer was still watching and wondering what was going on.

"So, where did you find my wallet, then?" said David.

"In the cemetery which isn't too far away from here," said Jordan.

"I walk my dog up there all the time, I could have lost my wallet there at any time in the last few days," said David.

"When was the last time you were up there?" said Jordan.

"About four o'clock yesterday afternoon. Come to think about it, I stopped and went into the shop that is just down the road and bought myself a bottle of water and I had my wallet then. So, can I have my wallet back please?" said David.

Jordan thought for a moment, then she decided to give him his wallet back. She had been going to give the wallet to the police and let them deal with David, but she decided against it. At least she knew where David lived and she would be keeping an eye on him to see if he had anything to do with the case. Anyway, David's story about walking his dog round the cemetery sounded a plausible one. At this point, Jordan decided to leave the questioning there and the three of them made their way out to the car. When the three of them were stood outside next to the car they had a little chat.

"So, what do you think?" said Jarvis.

"His story about walking his dog round the cemetery I find believable, but I will be keeping an eye on things to see if he is involved in the case or not," said Jordan.

"What would you like to do now?" said Carl.

"I would like to hang around here and see if David goes anywhere," said Jordan.

"Do you want me to stay with you?" said Jarvis.

"No, if you could go back to the bed and breakfast and I will call you when I need you," said Jordan.

At that, Jarvis and Carl got into the car and drove away while Jordan went to find somewhere where she could be out of sight, but still able to see David's static caravan. About thirty yards from David's caravan was a bench for Jordan to sit on. There was a tree between the bench and David's caravan, so it wasn't too obvious that Jordan was sat there.

Jordan had been sat there for almost an hour and a half and David never came out of his caravan. But just then, she saw something. She could see someone coming out of the caravan opposite David's. This person then started to walk towards Jordan. When this person walked past the bench where Jordan was sat, he lifted his head and looked at her. He seemed surprised to see her sitting there, but carried on walking off the caravan park. As he did so, something fell out of his pocket. Jordan went to pick up whatever it was so she could give it back to the person, but when she picked up the item she saw that it was a pocket watch. The first thing she thought was this must be the pocket watch killer, but before ringing for backup she wanted to make sure.

So, for now, Jordan forgot about David and started to follow the one who had dropped the watch, on the off chance he was the killer. Jordan didn't want to make it obvious that she was following him, so she just hung back slightly to see what he was up to. At first, it appeared that he was just out for a walk. Then, after about fifteen to twenty minutes it was obvious that he was heading towards the seafront. Here, there were several benches for people to sit on. The man chose an unoccupied bench and sat down. Several feet behind where the killer was sitting was a low wall and Jordan went and sat on it.

Even though Jordan had an idea that she was probably watching the killer, because of the pocket watch he had dropped, she wasn't sure of it just yet. As she was watching him, Jordan noticed that the killer appeared to be watching people who walked in front of him. It seemed that he was paying more attention to young women who were in their late teens to early twenties.

Then, a young lady, who appeared to be in her early twenties, came walking off the beach. This young woman the killer seemed really interested in. As she started to walk away he got up to follower her. Jordan then followed behind them to make sure the woman would be safe.

After about ten minutes the woman that the killer was following went into a café. While she was in the café the killer stayed outside and watched her, and Jordan watched the killer. The woman bought herself a coffee to take away, then, she came out of the café. She stood there for a moment and had a drink of her coffee, then when she began to walk away the killer followed her once more. Jordan followed the two of them, keeping a very close eye on what was happening.

Soon, they were heading away from the seafront to an area with a few houses dotted around; it seemed a real quiet area. The woman walked into what appeared to be a park area, where there were large lawn areas, paved footpaths leading in different directions and there were quite a lot of trees dotted around. Along the footpaths there were several benches for people to sit on. The woman went to one of these benches and sat down. She put her coffee down on the bench next to her, took out a book from a bag that she was carrying, opened the book at the relevant page and started to read. She was totally unaware that she was being watched.

The killer stood several feet directly behind the young woman so that she wouldn't see him and Jordan stood next to a nearby tree so the killer wouldn't see her. While Jordan was watching the killer, it seemed to her that the killer was preparing himself to attack the woman. But just as he was about to make his move, someone else came into view, walking on the path towards the woman who was sat on the bench. When the person reached the bench they sat down next to the woman. Then, by the way the two of them greeted each other it was obvious that they them knew each other. When the killer saw this he was obviously disappointed, so, he started to walk away the same way he had come. Jordan ducked out of the way, a little further round the tree that she was stood next to, so that he wouldn't see her.

As the killer walked past the tree, Jordan's mobile phone started to ring. But the killer didn't think anything of it because he thought it could be the woman's phone and he carried on walking. Once the killer was far enough away, Jordan started to follow him again and she also answered her phone.

"Hello," whispered Jordan.

"Hi, it's me. I was just wondering what you were up to," said Jarvis.

"I'm just following a lead and I can't really talk right now."

"I take it you are following someone, then?"

"Yes, I am. I will speak to you later," said Jordan.

At that, the two of them hung up. As Jordan put her phone away the killer went round a bend in the path. Jordan picked up her pace so that she could see him, but it was as if he had disappeared. There were several trees and bushes nearby and Jordan assumed he must be hiding behind one of them. So, Jordan started to look for him. But after almost twenty minutes of looking and not finding him she decided to go back to the bed and breakfast. Jordan called Jarvis and asked him to meet her where he had left her. What she didn't know was the killer was watching her walk away. When she was far enough away he came out from behind the bush he was hiding behind and started to walk in the other direction.

CHAPTER FOUR

―――

M eanwhile, Jane Brown, the CSI working on the case, was arriving at the station. When she was in the reception area a member of staff opened the door that allowed Jane to go upstairs to see Lucas, where she found him Lucas sitting at his desk. She could see the pocket watch and also that Lucas was on his computer. From what she could see, Lucas was looking at the reception area of the police station.

"So, you are trying to find who left the pocket watch, then?" said Jane.

"Yeah, he has to be here somewhere. And there he is, I've got him," said Lucas.

What Lucas could see was someone sat on the bench where he found the pocket watch and this person was holding the pocket watch. Now, he wanted to get the face of the potential killer out to the public, to see if anyone recognised him. He made up a lot of wanted posters to put in shop windows and on lamp posts around town. He also got several officers going from door to door asking people if they had seen this person. While he did this, Jane put the pocket watch into an evidence bag and took it back to the lab.

Within an hour or so Lucas had all the posters that he needed and there was a new shift of uniformed officers coming on duty. So, Lucas grabbed as many of the posters as he could to put up in shop windows and to go door to door.

Lucas wasn't one to sit around and do nothing. He kept some of the posters for himself and started to go door to door with the other officers. When Lucas had picked up his posters he then made his way to his car. All the other officers had their allocated areas and Lucas started at the caravan park where Jordan was earlier. There were two entrances to the caravan park and with Lucas coming to the caravans from a different direction to Jordan, he used the other entrance which was at the back of the caravan park. When he found a space to park his car, and get out he started to go from door to door.

The first few people he spoke to didn't know the person in the picture. But then, the next two or three seemed to recognise him and they had an idea that he could live somewhere near the front entrance. So, Lucas drove round to the front entrance and had a look around to decide which caravan to go to first. He chose one of the caravans nearest the entrance. As he walked over to the caravan, the killer walked through the front entrance. As he did so he noticed Lucas at David's caravan, instantly recognising him as the detective investigating the murder case. Near to where the killer was stood were a couple of large dumpsters, so the killer stood next to them in an attempt to hide and watched Lucas from there. When David opened the door both he and Lucas looked at each other for a moment.

"You're DS Lucas, aren't you?" said David.

"Yes, I am and I seem to recognise you from somewhere," said Lucas.

"Several years ago I was given a five year prison sentence for a string of robberies and you were the one who arrested me," said David.

"I remember now, you targeted newsagents if I remember correctly," said Lucas.

"Yeah, that's right," said David.

"So, anyway, the reason why I'm here today is because I am investigating the murders that have occurred recently. I have a photo here for you to look at and I was wondering if you recognised this person?" said Lucas.

David took the photo from Lucas and said, "So, this is the pocket watch killer that everyone is talking about, then. You know, this guy looks very much like the one who lives in the caravan over there."

"What, that one over there?" said Lucas, pointing.

"Yeah, that one," said David.

The killer was still stood at the dumpsters and he was close enough to hear what they were talking about. He was sure that David and Lucas were talking about him and his caravan. As Lucas was walking over to the caravan that David had pointed out, David called out to him.

"Do you know that there is a private investigator looking into the case?" said David.

"Yeah and how do you know this, then?" said Lucas.

"Because she came to see me earlier."

"Does this PI have a name, then?"

"Jordan Lewis," said David.

Lucas was really curious about a PI working on the case and would look into it the first chance he got. He then went over to the caravan that David had pointed out. All the while the killer was still watching. While he was watching he saw Lucas go to the static caravan that was next to his. He was really curious to know why he had gone to that caravan.

When Lucas knocked on the door he didn't get an answer, so he knocked again. Again, he received no answer. At this point, Lucas began to think that this person wasn't home. Lucas really needed to talk to this person, so, he decided to sit in his car and wait a while just in case they were on their way home. When the killer saw what Lucas was doing he began to wonder if he should take a chance by going back to his caravan. After he had thought about it for a moment, the killer decided to go back to his caravan. As he came from behind the dumpsters the killer could see that Lucas was doing something in his car and hadn't noticed him yet. But when he was a few feet from his caravan, Lucas looked up and noticed him. He compared it to the photo on the wanted poster. With the person of interest in the photo having his head down slightly Lucas couldn't see his face fully, but from what he could see this man looked similar. So, Lucas decided to have a chat with him. When the killer was in his caravan Lucas got out of his car.

When Lucas knocked on the door the killer looked out of the window. When he saw Lucas standing there he started to hear the voice again. "He knows, you have to do something," said the voice. He knew that Lucas would have seen him go into his caravan and it would look suspicious if he didn't open the door. So, the killer very slowly opened the door.

"Hi there, I was wondering if you could help me?" said Lucas.

"If I can," said the killer nervously.

"I am DS Lucas from the local police and I'm looking to talk to your neighbour in the next caravan. I was wondering if you knew where he is or when he will be back?" said Lucas.

"Well, as far as I know he goes out to work in the morning and he usually arrives home between half five and a quarter to six in the evening," said the killer.

"Okay, do you know where he works by any chance?" said Lucas.

"Sorry, but no, I have no idea," said the killer.

"Well, I can't think of anything else, thank you for your time. By the way, have we ever met before, because you seem really familiar?" said Lucas.

"No, I don't think so," said the killer.

At that, Lucas left the caravan and went back to his car. With it only being ten to three in the afternoon Lucas decided to come back at half five to talk to the person in the caravan. But before he left he called the station for a uniformed officer to come to his location to keep an eye on the caravan, just in case the person came home early. While he was in his car waiting for the other officer, Lucas sat there thinking. While he was thinking he had a look at the picture on the wanted poster that he had. He was trying to work out if the person he had just spoken to was the one in the picture.

While Lucas was sat in his car the killer was watching from his window. The killer was wondering why Lucas was just sitting there. "He's on to you," said the voice. "You are going to have to do something." Now, the killer was beginning to panic. He started to walk up and down the length of his static caravan, trying to think what to do. After a few minutes of pacing up and down he went and sat on his bed, picked up his box of pocket watches and started to sort through them. "Yeah, that's right, go and grab another victim," said the voice.

The killer put on his coat and shoes, put a pocket watch in his coat pocket and made his way out of his caravan. When he had locked the door he made his way off the caravan park. As he reached the exit a police car came driving in. The killer just put his head down, stood to one side to let the car pass, then, he walked off the caravan park. He decided to get away from the immediate area and to go to Newquay. The killer walked a few hundred yards to a bus stop and waited for the relevant bus. When he had been at the bus stop a few minutes Lucas came driving out of the caravan park. Lucas was heading back to the station and he had to drive past where the killer was waiting for a bus. As Lucas drove past the bus stop he looked at the killer and then again at the photo of the man sat in the police station's reception area, which was on the passenger seat. Now, Lucas wasn't sure if the person in the picture and the person stood at the bus stop were the same person.

As Lucas drove by, the killer saw the bus for Newquay travelling towards him. When the bus had stopped he got on, paid the fare for the journey and went and sat down by the window. As the bus travelled along its route the killer just looked out of the window but every time the bus arrived at a stop the killer watched to see who got on and off. One time when the bus stopped a young woman in her early twenties got on the bus. When she had paid her fare she found a seat about halfway up the bus on the left-hand side. The killer was sat two seats further back on the right-hand side. The young woman was also going to Newquay and for the rest of the journey the killer did nothing but watch her.

Before long the bus was arriving in Newquay. When the woman realised where they were, she got out of her seat and walked to the front of the bus in readiness to get off. The killer then got out of his seat and followed her to the front of the bus. When the bus had stopped and they had got off the killer started to follow the woman. After a few minutes of following the woman it appeared to the killer that she was heading towards the shopping area of Newquay. As they were walking along the road, a police car drove slowly by. When he saw the police car the killer slowed down and didn't make it obvious that he was following the woman. When the police car was far enough away the killer's full attention returned to the young woman. All the time the voice was saying to him, "She's the one."

Meanwhile, Lucas was arriving back at the station. When he was back at his desk and looked on his computer, he saw that he had an email from Jane, the CSI, asking him to call her as soon as he could. The first thing he thought was that it was about the pocket watch that was left in the reception area. So, he called her straight away.

"Hi Jane, it is Lucas. What do you have for me?" said Lucas.

"It's the pocket watch that I got from you, I got one fingerprint from it," said Jane.

"Yeah, did you get a name from it?" said Lucas.

"Yes, I did. It is an ex-con called David Crammer," said Jane.

As soon as Lucas heard the name David Crammer he ended the call with Jane, then grabbed his coat and car keys and made his way back to the caravan park.

Meanwhile, Jordan and Jarvis were arriving back at the bed and breakfast in St Ives. On the journey back to the bed and breakfast Jordan was really quiet. This told Jarvis that she wanted to be left alone to think things through. So, when they were inside Jordan went to her room and Jarvis went to his.

When she was inside her room Jordan went and sat on her bed and started to think about the person she had been following. Then, she remembered about the pocket watch that he had dropped. She put her hand in her right hand jacket pocket and pulled out the watch. As she sat there looking at the pocket watch she thought to herself that it must have been the killer that she had followed.

While she was thinking what her next move should be, Jordan turned on the TV that was in the room and went to lie down on the bed. For some reason, while she was working on a case and thinking about what to do, she always liked a bit of background noise to help her think. One thing she was thinking of doing was to go back to the caravan park and watch out for him for a while. But then she remembered that there were not many places where she could be out of sight. Then, what she started to consider was whether to talk to the local business owners like shops, hotels and bed and breakfasts to see what the local people knew about the case.

While she lay there deciding what to do, the local news came on the TV. So, she sat up to watch, to see if there was anything of interest. Then, after the news reader had been reading the news for a few minutes he was handed a piece of paper. On the piece of paper there was a new story. The new story was about the pocket watch killer case. There had been a body of a young woman found in Newquay which had been linked to the pocket watch killer. The news reader continued to say that the body had been found behind a row of shops on the seafront and the police were investigating.

Jordan knew she had to get to Newquay to see exactly what was going on. She put on her coat, grabbed her car keys and made her way into the corridor and across to Jarvis's room. When she knocked on the door it took Jarvis two or three minutes to answer.

"Sorry about that I was in the bathroom," said Jarvis.

"We need to get to Newquay," said Jordan.

"Why, what's happening in Newquay?"

"I've just been watching the local news and there has been a body found in Newquay which has been linked to the pocket watch killer. I want to go and have a look to see if I can get any clue to who the killer may be," said Jordan.

At that, Jarvis put on his shoes and coat and the two of them made their way to the car. Soon, they were in Jordan's car driving to Newquay. On the journey Jordan couldn't get to Newquay quickly enough. While they were travelling Jordan was beginning to wonder what exactly they would find. While travelling to any crime scene Jordan has always been curious about what she may find. This all started when she was in her early twenties, when she first joined the police. Soon, they were arriving in Newquay. Now, all they had to do was to find the crime scene. They drove around Newquay to see if they could find where the police activity was. After about twenty minutes of driving round, Jordan saw a car turning down what appeared to be an alley. When she looked at the car more closely it had some writing on it. From what she could read she knew that the person driving was a member of the police forensic team. So, the first chance she got, Jordan turned her car around. When Jordan arrived at the alley she parked her car.

Jordan locked the car and the two of them went walking down the alley. Jordan didn't really want to be caught up with the police, so when she got to the other end of the alley she peered round the edge of the wall to see exactly what was happening. When she looked she saw that there was a small area cordoned off. Inside the cordon was what appeared to be a body with someone attending to the body; Jordan assumed this was the pathologist. Also, there was someone else in the cordon. It was a man in his early to mid-forties; he was dressed in a shirt and tie, trousers and a jacket. Jordan assumed that this was the officer in charge of the case and she was right: it was Lucas that she saw in the cordon. There were three uniformed officers helping to keep the scene secure.

The car that Jordan saw turn down the alley was parked about ten to twelve feet in front of her. As she was looking at the car Jordan saw someone starting to get out of the car on the driver's side. This was Jane Brown, the CSI that was working on the case. When Jane was out of the car she went to the rear of the car and opened the boot. She took a case out and then closed the boot. Jordan knew that the case contained everything that a CSI needed to gather evidence. When Jane had what she needed she went across to where the body was, ducked under the crime scene tape and started to look for evidence. Both Jane and Lucas exchanged a few words but Jordan couldn't quite hear what was said. Jarvis watched from behind, he knew not to disturb her thinking.

While Jordan was watching, the body was moved from its position and taken to a black van. Jordan assumed the pathologist was taking the body to the morgue. When the body was in the back of the van and Mandy the pathologist was in the driver's seat, the van set off in Jordan's direction. Both Jordan and Jarvis stood to one side to let the van pass. As Mandy drove off, Lucas glanced over. As he did so he noticed Jordan and Jarvis. At first, Lucas thought they were newspaper reporters, but the more he looked the more he started to think that Jarvis looked a little too old to be a reporter and he seemed to recognise Jordan from somewhere. Then, Lucas realised. When he was on the beach with the third body, he remembered seeing her in the small crowd that had gathered there. So, while he had the chance, Lucas went across to have a chat with her. Once the van had passed them and they looked back to where the body had been, both Jordan and Jarvis saw Lucas walking towards them.

"Can I help the two of you?" asked Lucas as he reached them.

"No, thank you, we're fine. We were just wondering what all the commotion was about," said Jordan.

"I seem to remember you from another one of my crime scenes. You know the one, the one on the beach the other day. Also, I've been told that your name is Jordan Lewis and you're a private investigator. Would I be right in saying that?" said Lucas.

Jordan thought for a moment, then, she said, "Yes, that would be correct and let me guess, you've been talking to David Crammer."

"Yes, I have. Could you tell me who has employed you to look into the case?" said Lucas.

"I'd rather not. I prefer to keep my employer's name to myself," said Jordan.

"Okay, for now. But who's this with you?" said Lucas.

"This is Jarvis, a friend of mine. He's a retired criminologist who helps me with my cases," said Jordan.

"Okay, how about we swap contact details so we can keep each other updated about the case?" said Lucas.

At that they gave each other their business cards. When that was done Lucas walked back to the crime scene while Jordan and Jarvis were about to walk away. But just then Jordan glanced over to the crime scene and saw Jane, the CSI, pick up a pocket watch and put it in an evidence bag. It was then Jordan knew that this murder was the work of the pocket watch killer.

CHAPTER FIVE

O n the way back to the bed and breakfast, Jordan
was quiet. She was thinking about what she had just
seen. Then, she started to think about the person she had
followed from the caravan park, the one that had dropped
the pocket watch. She had a real good feeling that he
was involved, somehow, in the case. Then, Jordan decided
that she didn't want to go back to the bed and breakfast.
She asked Jarvis if he could ask his friend Carl where the
library was. Jordan wanted to go to the library so that she
could read some newspaper articles about the case.

Jarvis very quickly got through to Carl on the phone
and before long he had directions to the library. He, in
turn, gave Jordan the directions and before long they
were arriving at the library. When Jordan had parked her
car, the two of them made their way inside. Once inside,
Jordan asked a member of staff the whereabouts of the
newspapers. The staff member told her the newspapers
were upstairs, so the two of them made their way upstairs.

When the two of them were upstairs, they saw the
section they needed and they went across. They grabbed
a few newspapers each, sat down at a nearby table and
started to read. They read everything they could about

the case. In one newspaper articles, the reporter wondered if the recent murders had any connection to a couple of murders that had occurred nearly ten years ago. When Jordan read this she became really curious about those murders and wanted to read more about them.

Jordan went to find a member of staff and told her what she needed. Jordan was taken to a machine. With this particular machine you can put a micro film in and you can look at and read what you are interested in. Within a few minutes that staff member had put in the correct micro film and Jordan started to scroll through a lot of newspaper articles.

When Jarvis had finished reading his small pile of newspapers, he looked up and saw Jordan sat at the machine. Interested in what she was doing he walked across and sat down next to her. He could see that she was looking at some newspaper articles of ten years earlier.

"What are you looking for?" said Jarvis.

"I read in one of those newspapers over there that these recent murders could be connected to a couple of murders ten years ago. I am interested in knowing which murders," said Jordan.

Now, Jarvis was really interested in discovering which murders, if any, were linked. Unbeknown to the two of them, while they were looking through the articles the killer came walking in to the library. The killer was a member of the library as he really enjoyed reading. The killer remained on the ground floor level of the library, totally unaware that Jordan and Jarvis were upstairs. For the next fifteen to twenty minutes he looked along the shelves to choose a book. When he had chosen one he found a quiet spot, sat down at an empty table and started to read.

While he was doing that Jordan and Jarvis had found some newspaper articles about the murders of ten years earlier. Jordan asked a member of staff if she could have some printed copies of these articles so that she could read them more comfortably at the bed and breakfast. When she was given the printed copies and she had paid for them, both she and Jarvis began to make their way out of the library.

The killer was still sat at the table reading the book he had chosen. When they were downstairs Jarvis saw a sign that said the library was offering a temporary membership. Jarvis really enjoyed reading so he decided to take advantage of the offer. When Jarvis had sorted out his temporary membership he began to browse for a couple of books. In the meantime, Jordan sat at an empty table and started to look through the articles she just had printed off. She began to get a real uncomfortable feeling. It was the kind of feeling that she sometimes got when something was going to happen. So, she stopped reading the articles and went to find Jarvis.

Jarvis was in the fiction section. He was looking through some detective novels. By the time Jordan found him he had decided which two books he wanted to read, so he went to the desk to check them out. While he was doing that the killer was still sat at the table reading the book that he had chosen. For one brief second he glanced over to where Jordan and Jarvis were. Straight away he recognised Jordan and he knew he had to get out of there. The killer stood up, walked behind a book stand and started to make to make his way out of the library, using different book stands to hide behind so Jordan wouldn't see him. As he was making his way out of the library, Jordan glanced over towards the door and she caught a glimpse of him walking through the door.

Jordan was pretty sure this person was the one she had followed from the caravan park, but she wasn't one hundred per cent certain. She went to check to make sure, but before she did she quickly gave the articles she had printed out to Jarvis and then exited the library. At first, she couldn't see where the person had gone, then, she saw them in the distance. When she saw him she set off after him. When she was close enough she saw that it *was* the same person she had followed from the caravan park. Obviously, Jordan didn't know at this point that he was the killer, but she had a very good idea. So, she kept her distance and watched what he was up to, if anything.

A couple of times the killer looked behind him to see if Jordan was following him. Every time he looked round, Jordan made sure she was out of sight so he wouldn't see her. When he was a good distance away from the library and he thought Jordan wasn't following him, the killer became more relaxed.

While Jordan was following the killer, she glanced across the road and she saw David Crammer, who she had spoken to at the caravan park. David hadn't seen Jordan, but he saw the killer who he recognised as a neighbour from the caravan park. The first chance he got, David crossed the road to talk to him. Jordan knew that the killer lived in the caravan opposite, but she was curious to know what they were talking about.

Before long David and the man that Jordan was following were getting away from the busier areas to where it was much quieter. Soon, they were in wide open spaces where there were no houses or other buildings. Jordan had to be careful, because there weren't many places to hide if the two men ever turned round. For the next few minutes the two men carried on walking and talking and Jordan carried on following them. The next thing Jordan knew she was following the two men down a different path. This path had trees and hedgerows down both sides, it was also really narrow. Then, without warning, the two men stopped walking and they were just stood there talking. On the off chance that they might turn around, Jordan had to find somewhere to hide. Luckily there was quite a large bush two or three feet wide, so she got behind it as quickly as she could. She could see that she could get level with the two men without being seen and listen to what they were talking about.

Jordan knew she was getting closer to them because she could hear their voices more clearly with every step. Then, when she was almost level with them she stood on a twig which gave out a loud snapping sound. When the two men heard that they stopped talking and carried on walking. Jordan heard them start to walk off, so she waited several seconds, she then peered round the bush and saw them walking off. When they were far enough away she started to follow them again.

After a few minutes of walking they came across what appeared to be an old barn. To Jordan the two men didn't seem surprised to see the barn. As the two men walked towards the barn, Jordan stayed back in the shadows of a large tree and watched to see what they did next. From what she could see the two of them walked to the large doors which were locked with a thick, large chain and a padlock. While she was watching the killer took what appeared to be a key from his right-hand trouser pocket and unlocked the padlock. When he had done that he opened the barn door and the two of them went inside. When they were inside one of them pulled the door to but didn't completely close it.

When the two of them had been in the barn for a minute or so Jordan decided to get a little closer to see what the two of them were up to. Her curiosity always got the better of her. Jordan quietly made her way to the barn door, making sure she didn't stand on any more twigs as she did so. She peered through a gap in the door. When she looked in she could see that on the right-hand side of the barn it was filled with what looked like really old fashioned kind of furniture. It seemed to Jordan that it was the kind of furniture that someone would have in their house about a hundred years ago. The main piece of furniture that really stood out was a large wooden table with what appeared to be wooden chairs that went with it. Jordan couldn't see exactly how many chairs there were but there seemed to be a lot. Then, covering most of the remaining space there were some wooden packing cases. To Jordan it looked like someone had emptied a house and had put the contents in the barn. When Jordan looked towards the back wall of the barn, she saw someone standing there. With them having their back to her and with it being a little gloomy she couldn't quite see who it was. As she was wondering where the second man was she felt a sharp pain on the back of her head and she slumped to the floor unconscious.

By now, Jarvis was becoming concerned. He knew that Jordan was following a lead, but what concerned him was that he had heard nothing from her for about an hour. Jarvis didn't know where she was or if she was alright. Jarvis gave Jordan a call on her mobile but received no answer. Now, he was really concerned. Luckily, Jordan had left the car keys with him, so he decided to go for a drive around to see if he could find her.

Obviously Jarvis didn't know which direction Jordan had gone, so when he was in the car he started by having a drive round the general area of the library on the off chance he could spot her. After about ten minutes of driving round he thought that he had seen Jordan about a hundred yards in front of him, so he sped up a little to catch up with her. However, when Jarvis was level with her he saw that it wasn't Jordan, it was just someone who looked like her. So he carried on driving to look for her, going further afield as he did so.

After almost an hour and half of looking there was still no sign of her. Repeatedly during that time, Jarvis stopped the car and tried calling her, but with no success. Unbeknown to Jarvis he was heading in the right direction and was getting closer and closer to the barn where Jordan was. The road that Jarvis was travelling down was heading towards the path that led towards this barn. As Jarvis was driving towards the path he noticed someone walk out from the path, then, they started to walk towards Jarvis. When Jarvis was almost level with the person he saw that it was David Crammer. Jarvis had been with Jordan when she had spoken to David at his caravan, so, he knew exactly who David was.

Jarvis was really curious to know what David was up to and what was down the path that David was walking from. So, Jarvis stopped the car at the entrance of the path. Straightaway he saw that he wouldn't be able to drive the car down the path and he would have to walk if he wanted to explore. So, Jarvis got out of the car and locked the doors. As Jarvis was about to walk down the path he looked down the road in David's direction. David was still walking away and it appeared that he hadn't noticed Jarvis.

Now David was a good way away, Jarvis started to walk down the path. As he was walking down the path Jarvis was looking everywhere. He was totally unaware of what to expect. Then, he heard a snapping sound, as if someone had stood on a twig. With the area being covered in bushes and trees Jarvis couldn't see who or what had made the sound. After a moment or so of looking around to see where the sound had come from he carried on walking down the path.

All the time Jarvis was walking down the path he had an uncomfortable feeling. It was the kind of feeling as if he was being watched or followed. When he was nearly at the other end of the path he heard the snapping sound again. This time it really unnerved him. But when Jarvis had a look around, he still couldn't see anything.

By now, Jordan was beginning to come round. When she was fully awake and aware of her surroundings she realised that she was still at the barn doors with a very large headache. Then, she started to get to her feet. When she was on her feet she realised that she was still a little wobbly. Then, she started to think about what had happened to her. Jordan then realised that David Crammer and the killer could still be in the area. So, she started to check around her. The first place she wanted to check was the barn. When she looked at the barn doors she could see they were locked again with the chain and padlock. Jordan really wanted to have a look around the inside of the barn, so, she went to have a look for another entrance. As she set off to have a look Jarvis came walking off the path.

"So, there you are, are you okay?" said Jarvis.

"Yes, just a bit of a headache, how did you find me?" said Jordan.

"Just by chance really, what are you doing here, anyway?".

"When we were in the library and you were at the desk sorting your books out I saw someone leave. I saw this particular person on the caravan park. You know, when I stayed there after talking to David Crammer. Well, as I was following him David joined him when we were about halfway here. When we arrived here the one I was originally following unlocked the barn door and the two of them went inside. After a minute or so I came across to see what they were up to. I wasn't stood there long when I was knocked unconscious. The next thing I knew I was coming round and then you turned up."

"Do you think the person you followed from the library has anything to do with the case?" said Jarvis.

"I'm unsure," said Jordan. "Anyway, the reason why I came down this path in the first place is because I saw David Crammer at the other end."

"Yeah, if that's the case I wonder where the other person is."

At that, the two of them started to think this person, who actually is the killer, could still be in the area and could be watching them. They were right to think that, because about a hundred yards away and hiding behind a tree was the killer and he *was* watching them.

But, even with this in mind, Jordan still wanted to check out the barn. With one of the men sneaking behind her to hit her over the head Jordan knew there had to be another way into the barn somewhere. As they went down one side of the barn they could see there was no way in, but when they were round the back it was a different story: they found another door. Jordan expected the door to be locked but she went to check on the off chance that it was unlocked. The door was locked but there was a window next to it. When Jordan had a closer look at the window it looked like it might be unlocked. When she tried it, it was indeed unlocked and it was one of those windows that slid to one side, so she was able to climb through it. Then she turned and looked at Jarvis.

"I'll stay here and keep a look out, just in case someone comes back," said Jarvis.

At that, Jordan started to have a look around. Jordan was very careful as she walked around because she was still unsure if there was anyone still in the barn. As Jordan was walking to the front of the barn she could see the things that she had seen from the front door. Then, something caught her eye. On her right hand side Jordan noticed a work bench that was next to the wall. On top of the bench there was a smallish box and Jordan was curious to know why this box was by itself. So, she walked across to have a look. When she looked in the box, Jordan could see that it was about half full with pocket watches. Jordan was now even more convinced that at least one of the two men she had followed to the barn was the pocket watch killer.

Meanwhile, while Jordan was looking round the barn, the killer, who was still watching from behind the tree, was now really curious about what Jordan was doing. So, he decided to move from his position to see, if he could, what Jordan was up to, making sure he stayed hidden the best he could.

While the killer was making his way to the barn to see what Jordan was doing, Jordan had finished looking round the barn. Apart from the box of pocket watches there was nothing else of interest to her. So, she went back to the window, climbed back out and closed the window to how it was before. At that point, both Jordan and Jarvis started to walk away. The killer saw them but he didn't want to attract attention to himself, so, he hid next to a nearby tree and watched them walk away.

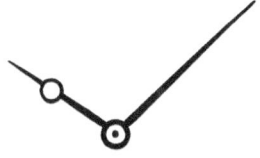

CHAPTER SIX

———

I t had just turned four o'clock in the afternoon and Lucas was sat at his desk thinking about the case. Lucas had been out for a few hours going from door to door. He had the image he had got off the CCTV of the person who had left the pocket watch in the reception area, but no one recognised him.

Lucas had started work at about five o'clock that morning, so he decided to call it a day and made his way home. He picked up his case file and made his way downstairs to his car. On his way down to the car park he was thinking about the man who had left the pocket watch. Lucas thought it would be a good idea to have a drive around the area on his way home, on the off chance he saw the person in question.

Lucas started by having a drive round St Ives. One of the killer's victims had been found on the beach in St Ives and he knew that a lot of offenders returned to the crime scene. So, he knew it was possible he could come across the person he was looking for.

With it being a warm, sunny afternoon there were a lot of people out and about, most of whom were tourists. As he was driving through the tourist areas of St Ives he didn't see the person he was looking for and nothing seemed to be out of place. So, Lucas decided to go to the quieter parts of St Ives where it was less likely to find tourists. Lucas knew that most offenders preferred quieter areas because it would be less likely for them to be seen if there were fewer people around.

After about an hour and a half of driving around the quieter area of St Ives without seeing the person he was looking for, Lucas decided to drive on to Penzance, where another one of the killer's victims had been found. On the passenger seat next to Lucas he had a police radio. While he was travelling to Penzance a call came over the radio from the control room that there had been another body found in Truro and it could be linked to the pocket watch killer. Lucas got straight on to the radio and asked the control room where exactly in Truro the body was. When he had the precise location Lucas made his way to Truro.

At the same time, Carl Benson, Jarvis's friend, was listening to the police channel on his scanner. He heard everything about the body being found in Truro, even the location. When he had written this down he gave Jarvis a call.

Jordan and Jarvis were just arriving back at the bed and breakfast when Jarvis received the call from Carl. When Carl had finished telling Jarvis what he had heard on his scanner, Jordan wanted to get to Truro as soon as she could, but she didn't know how to get there. With Carl knowing the area very well it was arranged for him to pick them up from the bed and breakfast and take them there.

Soon, Carl was arriving at the bed and breakfast and Jordan and Jarvis were outside waiting. While they were

travelling to Truro Jordan was wondering if the body that
was found there was anything to do with the pocket watch
killer. Jordan was thinking that for the killer to get from
the barn to Truro and kill someone, he would have had
to move very quickly. But she didn't say anything to Jarvis
or Carl just yet because she wanted to take a look at the
body and crime scene first.

As they were about to enter Truro Jordan suddenly
got a feeling of dread come over her! Whenever Jordan
got this, she knew that more often than not there was
something going to happen and it was usually something
to do with the case.

Soon, they were arriving at the crime scene. Carl
didn't park the car too close to the scene because he didn't
want to get in the way of the police. As they got out of the
car they could see the area round the body was already
cordoned off. Jarvis and Carl stayed with the car but
Jordan went for a closer look. When she was close enough
Jordan could see that Mandy Fletcher, the pathologist, was
already there taking care of the body. Jordan had a look
around the scene and a walk to see if she could find any
clues. The main thing she was looking for was a pocket
watch, but wherever she looked she couldn't see one. When
she was in a better position to have a look at the body she
couldn't see a pocket watch on or near the body either.

While Jordan was having a look around Lucas arrived
at the scene. At first, he didn't notice Jordan, Jarvis or
Carl. The first place Lucas went to was the body. While
Mandy, the pathologist, was dealing with the body, Lucas
had a quick look on and around the body. What he was
looking for was a pocket watch, but he couldn't see one.

"Does this one feel a little different to you?" said Lucas.

"Yes, it does. When I came here I was expecting another victim of the pocket watch killer, but I don't think she is," said Mandy.

"Yeah, I know what you mean. I can't see a pocket watch anywhere and for some reason it just feels different," said Lucas.

While they were talking, Jane Brown, the CSI, arrived at the scene. Jane got her evidence collecting kit out of the back of the van and started to look for evidence. While all this was going on Jordan had finished having a look around. She didn't find anything of interest that could have connected this body with the case, so, she went back to where Jarvis and Carl were standing. While she was walking back to them Jordan noticed that Lucas had arrived at the scene. As Jordan got to the car Lucas looked across and saw her, then went across to have a chat with her.

"Hi Jordan, what are you doing here?" said Lucas.

"Hi, I heard about the body here and I was wondering if it had anything to do with the pocket watch killer."

"And how did you hear about the body?"

"That would be me. I heard about the body on my scanner," said Carl.

Lucas looked at Carl with a quizzical stare and said, "You seem familiar – do I know you from somewhere?"

"You should, I'm Professor Carl Benson. I'm a retired criminologist and I've worked with the police for many years, yourself included," said Carl.

"Yes, I should've remembered. So, what's your interest in the case?" said Lucas.

"Because I'm a criminologist I have an interest in the criminal mind, but there is something about this case that has stuck with me."

"So, do you have any ideas about the body we've found here?" Lucas asked Jordan.

"I'm not sure. For some reason it doesn't feel to me to be the work of the pocket watch killer."

"Yeah, that's the feeling we get as well," said Lucas.

The four of them talked for a little while longer, then Jordan, Jarvis and Carl made their way back to the bed and breakfast. But Jordan didn't want to be inside and doing nothing, she wanted to be out trying to solve the case so Jordan told Jarvis and Carl that she was going for a drive on her own.

While she was driving around, Jordan had the time to think about the case and what her next move should be. She had not been driving long when she realised there was something in her left hand pocket of her jacket. When she put her hand in the pocket and pulled out the item she saw that it was a pocket watch. Then, she remembered. When she was at the caravan park a couple of days earlier with Jarvis, when she spoke to David Crammer, she had stayed behind by herself to see what David would do after their chat. While she watched David's caravan, one of his neighbours came out of his caravan and the pocket watch fell out of his pocket.

So, Jordan decided to drive to the caravan park on the off chance that David's neighbour was there. While on her way to the caravan park, Jordan was thinking about what had happened to her while investigating the case. When Jordan first arrived in Cornwall and saw someone in the alley next to the bed and breakfast, she was sure that it was David's neighbour. When she followed David to the barn he was with his neighbour. When she read all the information about the case that Carl had given her, the description of a potential suspect seemed to fit David's neighbour.

Soon, Jordan was at the caravan park. When she turned onto where the caravans were, she saw straight away the caravan where David's neighbour lived. A little way away she noticed a police car with a couple of officers sat inside. To Jordan they seemed to be watching the same caravan that she was interested in. With the police being there watching that particular caravan, Jordan assumed that Lucas shared the same suspicions. But Jordan knew if the one who lived in that caravan was the pocket watch killer or was involved with the case, he wouldn't risk coming back to the caravan with the police being there. So, she just drove on. As Jordan drove round the caravan park she came across the back entrance. So, she decided to go out that way instead of the front entrance.

As she was about to drive through the exit someone came walking in. This person was wearing a hooded sweatshirt with the hood over their head. Because of the hood, Jordan couldn't get a clear look at the person's face, but they seemed to be acting suspiciously and Jordan wanted to know. As soon as she drove out of the exit she parked her car and walked back in to the caravan park.

As soon as she was back on the caravan park she saw the person. Jordan noticed that they were walking towards where the police car was parked. So, Jordan started to follow them. When they arrived at where the police car was, the person Jordan was following suddenly stopped. They just stood there for a moment or so as if he didn't know what to do. To their left, but set back a little, was a caravan so the person went and stood by it. When the person turned to walk towards the caravan, they turned just enough for Jordan to get a clear look at their face. Jordan saw that it was the person she had followed earlier, who was actually the killer.

As the killer peered round the caravan at the police another police car came into view. The police that had just come in to view were there to relieve the ones already there. While he was stood there watching the police, the killer started to hear the voice again. "They are waiting for you. You can't go back to your caravan. What are you going to do?" said the voice. The killer was becoming visibly concerned with the police being there. "What are you going to do, think, think," said the voice. The more the voice spoke to him the more concerned the killer became.

With the killer's body language Jordan could tell he was becoming agitated. Just then, Jordan's mobile phone started to ring. As soon as he heard the phone the killer immediately turned around to see where it was coming from. As soon as he saw Jordan he recognised her and he knew he was in a bit of a tight spot. "Now, what are you going to do?" said the voice. The killer looked at Jordan then he looked at the police and then back to Jordan. "Don't just stand there, do something," said the voice. At that, the killer made a run for it. Jordan ignored her ringing phone and started to give chase.

The officers that were there saw Jordan chasing someone. They wondered if it had anything to do with why Lucas had posted them there in the first place, so they went to check it out. Two of the officers followed on foot and the other two drove the cars. When the officers were off the caravan park they soon saw which direction Jordan and the killer were going. Lucas had told the officers that there was a female private investigator looking into the case and they wondered if this was her.

While they were chasing the killer, he ducked down an alley behind a row of houses. Before Jordan and the two officers that were on foot came down the alley the killer had just enough time to get into one of the back yards. While he was in the yard getting his breath back he heard Jordan and at least two officers come into the alley. While he was stood there and listened, he heard Jordan briefly introduce herself and explain why she was there. Then, the killer realised he had to get out of there, hopefully without being seen. The first thing he did was to look at the house. When he looked through the back window the house seemed empty. "Go on, try the door. See if it's unlocked," said the voice. To his surprise the door was unlocked. At that point, the killer very quickly and very quietly went into the house and shut the door behind him.

The killer knew that the police would be there in numbers and start going from door to door in an attempt to find him. When he went to the front room he could see through the front window. Before he got too close to the window he saw two police cars pull up outside. When the officers got out of the cars, the killer realised that they were the ones from the caravan park. One of the officers was talking on his radio and then the two of them went running round to the alley. At that, the killer went to the window. When he looked he couldn't see anyone else out there. "If you are going to get out of this house then get out now!" said the voice. He went to the door and paused for a moment. Then, he opened the door and peered out. When he saw again that no one was there he got out of the house and left the area as quickly as he could. When he was away from the house and he realised that nobody was following him, the killer calmed down and started to think about what he should do next.

While the killer was making his way out of the area, Jordan, with the help of the four officers that were there, started to search the back yards. They were totally unaware that the killer had already got away. One of the officers gave Lucas a call. He told Lucas what was happening and where they were. When Lucas heard about what was happening he made it to their location with a small team of officers to help with the search.

Jordan began by checking the back yard next to the one the killer went in. When she looked over this particular wall she couldn't see the killer and everything appeared undisturbed. Luckily the walls weren't too high and Jordan was able to look over them. When Jordan looked into the next yard she didn't see anything out of place, but when she glanced through the window she saw the house could possibly be empty. Jordan stood there and thought for a moment. Then, she took a chance and went into the yard. She went to the window and looked in. When she looked in she could see that it was the kitchen, but she couldn't see a fridge, a freezer or a cooker. This also suggested to her that the house was empty.

Then, she turned to the back door. As she did so she noticed it was slightly ajar. Now, Jordan was thinking the killer could be using this house as a hideout. For a moment Jordan stood there and pondered. She knew that she had to check out the house to see if the killer was in there or not. So, she took a deep breath and impulsively went inside alone. From the kitchen Jordan slowly made her way in to the next room which was the living room. It was completely empty. She then made her way upstairs to check it out. Upstairs there were two bedrooms and a bathroom. She very slowly went into each room to check them out, but they were also empty with no sign of the killer. Jordan had now come to the conclusion that the killer had made his escape through the house. When Jordan came downstairs and looked out of the front window she saw a few police cars pulling up outside of the house. She noticed Lucas getting out of one of them, so she went out to talk to him.

Lucas saw Jordan coming out of the house and said, "So, what's going on here, then?"

"I'm sure that I am on to the killer and followed him here," said Jordan.

"So, it looks like the killer could be the one from the caravan park after all."

"Yeah it does, but it looks like he's got away."

"How did that happen?"

Jordan explained how and why they chased the killer to where they were. She also explained about the house with the unlocked back door and how the killer must have had some luck and found it.

"So, this person, who we believe could be the killer, used the house to escape through?" said Lucas.

"That's what I believe," said Jordan.

"Well, what do you think we should do next?"

Jordan suggested that Lucas maintain a couple of officers at the caravan park to keep an eye on the killer's caravan. She went on to explain about the barn that she had followed the killer to. Lucas was really interested in this barn and wanted to have a look at it so he took Jordan back to her car and then followed her to the barn.

They couldn't drive down the path to the barn because it was too narrow, so, they parked their cars at the end of the path and walked the rest of the way. As they did so, Jordan told Lucas why she had followed the killer here in the first place and what had happened to her. Within a few minutes they were at the barn. Instead of telling Lucas what she had seen and found inside the barn, she decided to show him. She went to the back of the barn and Lucas followed. When they were round the back Jordan tried the window and it was still unlocked. So, she opened it as far as it would go and started to climb in. As she was climbing through the window Lucas had a quizzical expression on his face, but as soon as Jordan had climbed through the window he followed her inside. Once the two of them were inside Jordan started to show Lucas what she had found. The first thing she wanted to show him was the box with the pocket watches inside.

"I am convinced these belong to the killer," said Jordan.

"From what you've told me I would have to agree," said Lucas.

The two of them started to have a look around the barn to see if they could find anything else of interest; Jordan took one side of the barn and Lucas took the other.

Jordan felt more comfortable having a look around the barn with Lucas being there, because if the killer came back Lucas would deal with him. The bang on the head she had received earlier had shaken her up a little more than she thought it would, well, at least more than she would admit to.

After a few minutes of looking around Lucas noticed a set of drawers, so, he went over to have a look. There were a few items on top, but nothing of interest to the case, so he began to look through the drawers, starting with the top drawer. When he opened the top drawer he saw that there were some small items, but when he rummaged around he realised that there wasn't anything of interest. He closed the top drawer and opened the next one down. The first thing Lucas spotted was what appeared to be a smallish photo album. Just out of curiosity Lucas picked up the album to have a look and started to flip through the photos. As he did so he came across a photo of the first victim. As he looked more closely at each photograph he realised that there were photos of all the victims in the album.

"Hey, come and have a look at this," Lucas said to Jordan.

"What have you found?"

"I've just found this photo album and you know what, there are photos of all the victims in here."

"I wonder if he selects his victims in advance and then he takes a photo of them as a reminder," said Jordan.

"If that's the case, then all these people in this album are potential victims," said Lucas.

"If that's the case then we have our work cut out for us."

Lucas wanted to see if there was any information on the back of the photos that would give a clue to who the people were. He had a pair of latex gloves in his coat pocket and he put them on before he touched the photos. As he took each photo out of the album to have a look at the back of them Jordan stood beside him and watched. But none of the photos had anything written on the back. Just then, Lucas stopped and paid more attention to one photo in particular. Straight away Jordan noticed this.

"You've spotted something, then?" said Jordan.

"Yeah, this woman here, she's an officer at my station," said Lucas.

The first thing Lucas did was to call the station to see if she was on or off duty. For the next few moments while the station were checking where the officer was, the phone line was fairly quiet. All Lucas could hear were the other officers talking and the tapping sounds of computer keyboards being used. Then, the officer came back on the line to inform Lucas that the officer in question was off duty. Lucas said that he wanted her found and brought to the station, but for now he didn't say why.

While the officer was being found and brought to the station, Jordan and Lucas continued to search the barn. Totally unaware that the police and Jordan were at the barn, the killer was making his way there, with the voice working overtime. "Well, you can't go back to the caravan because the police are watching it. So, what are you going to do? Come on now think, think," said the voice. The killer started to think about finding himself another victim. "That's right, you need another victim. You get yourself to the barn as quickly as you can and choose the right pocket watch," said the voice.

Before long the killer was getting close to the barn. As he was approaching the path, the one that led to the barn, he saw a couple of cars parked there, one of which was a police car. "See, even the police know about the barn. Now what are you going to do?" said the voice. While the killer decided what to do next he got himself off the road and hid behind a nearby tree so he wouldn't be seen. After a moment or so of thinking, the killer wanted to see exactly what was going on at the barn, so he made his way to the barn through the trees.

"I bet that woman has something to do with this, you know the one, that PI," said the voice. When he got to the barn the killer did not want to get too close and he hid behind a large tree so no one could see him. As he looked round the area of the barn he couldn't see anyone from his position. Then, he started to wonder if the police were round the back. When he felt ready, the killer made his way round to the back of the barn, but ensured he stayed within the treeline so no one would see him. He couldn't see anyone round the back either but spotted that the window was open. At that point, he knew they were inside. "They're inside going through your things, what are you going to do about that?" said the voice.

For a moment, the killer stood there trying to decide what to do. He really wanted to know what they were up to, so he took a chance and slowly made his way to the window, being careful not to make a sound because he didn't want anyone to know that he was there. When he got to the window he stood to one side of it and then he peered into the barn. As he looked in he saw Jordan and Lucas who were at the far end of the barn having a look around. "They're looking for evidence against you," said the voice.

While he was watching them Jordan and Lucas started talking, but they were too far away from the killer for him to be able to hear what they were saying. Then, Jordan looked in the direction of the window and the killer had to move back quickly. When he looked back through the window it was obvious that Jordan hadn't seen him because she was still having a look round the barn. While he was watching the two of them, the killer could hear voices coming from the other side of the barn. Then, he heard someone call out Lucas's name. Lucas replied to them, told them where he was and to come round to the back of the barn. When he heard that the killer very quickly got himself out of sight.

When the killer had got himself out of sight, he hung around to see what was happening. As soon as he'd done so two police officers appeared at the back of the barn. As the two of them walked towards the window, Lucas appeared at the window from the other side. Lucas said something to the officers then he started to climb through the window, followed by Jordan. The four of them made their way to the front of the barn totally unaware that they were being watched by the killer. The killer made his way to the front using the treeline to hide behind so he wouldn't be seen. When he was round the front he could see the four of them stood talking. Then, Jordan and Lucas left and the two officers stayed behind. "The police are even keeping an eye on this place, what are you going to do now?" said the voice.

The killer knew he needed some things from the barn, so while the two officers were at the front of the barn the killer went to the back. When he was at the back he waited a moment, then, when he was happy the officers weren't coming to the back, he made his way to the barn and through the window. "It will not be long before they will be checking the back, so hurry and grab what you need," said the voice.

The first thing he went for was the box of pocket watches. Near the box was a roll of tape. He used some of the tape and put it across the top of the box to make it secure. Then, just a few feet away from where he was standing were a large bag and a large rucksack. He picked up the bag and put it on the bench. When he opened the bag it was filled with clean clothes but there was just enough room for the box of watches. When he fastened the bag up, he put the rucksack on the bench. Inside the rucksack was a tent big enough for one. Also inside was a metal plate and cup along with a plastic knife, fork and spoon. Tied to the bottom of the rucksack was a sleeping bag. Down one side of the bench was an empty canvas bag; he put it on the bench and opened it. A few feet behind the bench were several tins of soup along with tinned potatoes and beans. He put in as many tins as he could carry into the bag as well as a small camping stove and a pan so he could warm up the food. He also took a tin opener.

When he had everything he needed he picked up the bags and made his way towards the window. When he was almost at the window he heard some voices. Straight away he put the bags down and he stood next to a large wardrobe. From where he was stood, he could see through the window but it would be difficult for anyone to see him. Then, he saw the two officers that Lucas had left to watch the barn. One of them came to the window and looked in. After a moment or so of looking around, the officer walked away from the window. The killer could still hear them talking but their voices were slowly fading away. When he couldn't hear their voices any more he went to the window and peered out to see if he could see them. When he was happy that they were back round the front he grabbed his bags and put them outside, then, he climbed through the window. When he was outside he picked up his bags and made his way out of the area.

CHAPTER SEVEN

—

David Crammer was sat in his caravan watching TV. When he had finished watching the programme that he was interested in, he turned off the TV, made a cup of coffee then he went and sat on the doorstep of his caravan for a while. He could see that the police car was still parked there. When he had arrived home earlier he had noticed them for the first time. David also noticed that they seemed to be watching the caravan opposite his. While he was sat on his doorstep drinking his coffee, one of the officers got out of the car and started to walk towards him.

"Excuse me, sir, would it be possible to use your toilet please?" said the officer.

"Of course you can, I'll show you where it is," said David.

While the officer was using the toilet, David finished his coffee and rinsed his cup out. When the officer had finished he thanked David for the use of the toilet and he went back to the car. All the time David was wondering where his neighbour was, because he hadn't seen him for a while.

With it being a nice afternoon and with having nothing else to do, David decided to go for a walk. In the meantime,

Jordan was in her room at the bed and breakfast. She was becoming really frustrated because she could feel that she was really close to the killer, but not close enough to grab him. Jordan didn't feel like being stuck inside, so she also went to get some fresh air, checking first if Jarvis would like to accompany her. Jarvis opened the door as Jordan was about to knock.

"I was about to go out for a walk and I was wondering if you would like to come?" said Jordan.

"That sounds like a good idea," said Jarvis.

Jordan wanted to go to the nearby beach, where one of the victims had been found. Revisiting the crime scene always helped her think about the case and get into the mind of the killer. Soon, they were approaching the beach. Even though it was late in the afternoon there were still a few people enjoying the beach. To Jordan they all seemed blissfully unaware of the recent murders that she was investigating. There was a low wall between the beach and the footpath, so Jordan went and sat on it. Parked nearby was an ice-cream van.

"I'll go and get us an ice-cream," said Jarvis.

Jordan smiled, then, she sat there thinking about the case. She played everything she knew through her mind, trying to make sense of it all. At the same time, Jordan was looking at the people on the beach and she noticed that a few of the women seemed similar in appearance to the victims in the case. "If they only knew," Jordan thought to herself. She then realised if people did know what could happen to them, then they would never leave their homes.

While Jordan was in her daydream Jarvis came back with the ice-creams. At first, Jordan didn't notice him, so when he handed her ice-cream to her it made her jump a little. While they ate their ice-creams they sat there quietly.

When the two of them had finished their ice-creams they went for a walk on the beach. With Jordan being so quiet, Jarvis knew she was thinking about the case, so he wouldn't talk unless she spoke to him first. They were getting closer and closer to the sea. On her feet all Jordan was wearing was a pair of sandals. So, when she got to the sea she took her sandals off and went for a paddle. Jarvis couldn't be bothered taking his shoes and socks off, so he stayed where he was, dry. Just then, a woman gave out a very loud scream. When Jordan and Jarvis looked across they saw a young couple chasing each other on the beach. But when she'd heard the scream the first thing Jordan thought of was the pocket watch killer.

With the police watching the killer's caravan Jordan thought to herself that he probably didn't have anywhere else to go. She knew that this would make it more difficult to find him. Now, Jordan was a little fed up with paddling and she came out of the sea. She left her sandals off for a while to give her feet time to dry. As they were walking back to where they came from, Jordan saw someone in the distance that seemed familiar. The person was stood on the beach near to where Jordan and Jarvis had sat to eat their ice-creams. When Jarvis glanced at Jordan he could see that she was looking at someone.

"Who are you looking at?" said Jarvis.

"That guy over there, the one wearing blue jeans and a grey jacket," said Jordan.

When Jarvis looked across he could see who she meant. When they got a little closer they could see that it was

David Crammer. Jordan didn't go and talk to David straight away – she wanted to see what he was up to first. At first, it appeared that David was just getting some fresh air and enjoying the weather, like them. But Jordan knew appearances could be deceiving.

David hadn't seen Jordan or Jarvis, and Jordan wanted to keep it that way. This was because she wanted to see if he was up to anything. Now, David started to walk away from them and they began to follow him. When they had been walking for a few minutes, two police officers came into view. When David saw the officers he didn't seem unsettled at all, not even a little bit. The two officers didn't seem to be in a rush or to be looking for anyone. This suggested to Jordan that they were just walking the beat.

While they were following David, Jordan could hear other people around her talking. She heard one person say that another dead body had been found, and the first thing she thought was, is it connected to the pocket watch killer. While they were following David, Jordan was trying to listen to what other people were saying. Then, Jarvis got a call on his mobile: it was his friend Carl. Carl had heard about the dead body on his police scanner and he knew where the body was. What Carl wanted to know was if Jordan would like to have a look around where the body was. When Jarvis asked her she said yes. Carl said that he would be at the bed and breakfast as soon as he could to pick them up. At this point, the two of them stopped following David and made their way back to the bed and breakfast.

While they were walking back to the bed and breakfast Jordan was wondering if this crime scene was going to be any different to the last one, where it didn't appear to be the work of the pocket watch killer.

Soon, the two of them were arriving back at the bed and breakfast. As they reached there, Carl pulled up in his car. On their way to Penzance, Carl told them what he knew. From what Carl had heard over his police scanner he felt it likely this victim was the work of the pocket watch killer.

While the three of them were making their way to Penzance, Lucas had been told about the body and was already on his way to the scene; he was wondering if he would ever solve this case. This case was now really beginning to frustrate him. With the amount of evidence he was confident that he would be able to get a conviction, all he needed to do was catch the killer.

Before long he was arriving at the crime scene. Straight away he could see that Mandy Fletcher, the pathologist, was already there. When he had parked his car and turned off the engine, Lucas, for a little while, just sat there and watched what was going on. The body was at a children's playground with swings, slides and a climbing frame. Lucas thought to himself if the killer dumps his victims in a children's playground then he really needs to get them off the streets as soon as possible.

While he was sat there, Jane Brown, the CSI, pulled up behind him. When she was out of his car Jane got the evidence collecting kit from the back seat. As she passed Lucas's car she smiled and gave him a wave. As she ducked under the crime scene tape she saw Mandy dealing with the body. Before Jane looked for evidence in earnest she had a casual look around the scene to see if anything caught her eye. As she looked around the scene her eyes slowly made their way to the body and she noticed something shining about three or four feet away from it. Jane was sure it wasn't anything to do with Mandy, so she went across to see what it was: when she arrived she saw that it was a pocket watch.

"Have you moved this here?" said Jane.

"No, it was there when I got here and the officers that are here swear that they haven't touched it," said Mandy.

"Looks like our good friend the pocket watch killer's been at it again," said Jane sarcastically.

"It certainly looks like it," said Mandy.

Jane took a photo of the watch in its position, then she put it in an evidence bag and put it away safe. As she was dealing with the watch Lucas also noticed it and he wanted a closer look. He was soon out of his car and walking across to Jane. When he reached Jane she showed him the watch.

"So, this is the work of the pocket watch killer, then?" said Lucas.

"Certainly seems so," said Jane.

"The manner of death appears the same, but I will be certain after the autopsy," said Mandy.

While they were talking, Jordan, Jarvis and Carl turned up at the scene. Before she'd even got out of the car, Jordan could see the evidence bag in Jane's hand with the pocket watch in the bag. Before she got out of the car Jordan had a glance round the scene to see if there was any evidence near the car. There wasn't any, so she got out of the car for a better look around. By now, Lucas had noticed that Jordan was at the scene. This didn't seem to bother Jordan, she just carried on looking for evidence. While she was walking around, she spotted something. When she had walked across she could see that it was a man's wallet. She knew she couldn't touch it, so she told Lucas what she had found. Both Lucas and Jane walked over to Jordan to see what she had found.

"You've found something, then?" said Lucas.

"Yeah, I've found this wallet," said Jordan.

Jane was the only one to be wearing latex gloves, so she bent down and picked up the wallet. When Jane opened the wallet she could see the ATM card was in the name of David Crammer.

"The wallet belongs to David Crammer," said Jane.

"Well, he does really like losing his wallets in the strangest of places," said Lucas.

Both Jordan and Lucas knew that they needed a really good talk with David and decided to go together. Jordan told Jarvis and Carl what was happening, then she got into Lucas's car to go and talk to David. Jarvis and Carl decided to follow them just in case they could be of assistance.

While they were on their way to see David, the killer had found somewhere to pitch his tent. He had found a little out of the way place a few short miles away from his caravan. He pitched his tent in this area so he would be hidden and it wouldn't be obvious that he was there. He was beginning to feel hungry, so he had a look to see what he fancied.

Now that he had committed another murder and he had another victim, he felt more relaxed. The voice in his head was quiet, for now. He decided on a tin of steak and a tin of potatoes for his meal. The food was soon warmed up with the camping stove and pans. While he was eating his meal the killer saw something move several feet in front of him. At first, he couldn't see what it was, but when it came into view he could see that it was a rabbit. It was soon joined by a second rabbit.

While he ate his meal the killer quite happily watched the rabbits. When he had finished eating he noticed two people a little way in the distance. At first, he wondered if they were the police, but when they got a little closer the killer realised that they were ramblers or bird watchers. As he watched them the couple were looking through binoculars and taking photos. Then, the two of them noticed the killer sitting in front of his tent.

"Hello there," said one of them.

"You've picked a nice place to camp," said the other.

"Have you heard about all of these murders, isn't it terrible?" said the first.

The two of them carried on talking and not really giving the killer a chance to say anything. But it appeared to him that they didn't know that he was the killer. "You can't let them leave, they will tell the police where you are," said the voice. This time the killer forced himself to ignore the voice. He was quite certain that the two ramblers weren't a threat and wouldn't tell the police. After a few minutes the two ramblers said goodbye to the killer and started to walk away. "You are doing the wrong thing by letting them go. They are going to tell the police," said the voice. But the killer once again ignored the voice.

While the killer was relaxing after his meal, Jordan and Lucas were arriving at the caravan park to talk to

David Crammer. When Lucas had parked his car, Carl, who had Jarvis with him, parked behind Lucas and a police car with two officers inside parked behind Carl. When they were out of the car Jordan and Lucas went to see if David was at home. While they did that the two officers got out of their car just in case their assistance was needed. The two officers that were already there watching the killer's caravan were curious to know what was going on, so they got out of their car to find out. Lucas briefly told them what was going on and then he knocked on the door. When he didn't get an answer he knocked again. While they were stood there waiting, Jordan remembered that she saw David on the beach and she told them about it. As they were talking about what they should do next, David came walking onto the caravan park. When David saw Jordan, Lucas and everyone else standing there, he knew that he had a problem.

"Can you come here, David, we need to have a chat with you," said Lucas.

"What is it all about this time?" said David.

"I'll tell you all about it when we get to the station," said Lucas.

Lucas decided to call off surveillance on the killer's caravan and they all returned to the station, along with David. All the way to the station David was wondering what all the fuss was about. Soon, they were arriving at the station. Jarvis told Jordan that he and Carl would wait in the car for her. When they were inside, David was put into a holding cell. While they waited for a duty solicitor to sit in with David on the interview, Jordan and Lucas had a chat about the case.

"Something doesn't feel quite right to me – what do you think?" said Lucas.

"You're right something is a little off with this. I also think finding the wallet is a little too convenient," said Jordan.

Soon, the duty solicitor had arrived and David was taken from the holding cell and transferred to an interview room. When they had given David and his solicitor a few minutes, both Jordan and Lucas went in to interview David.

"Why am I here?" asked David.

"Because we found something of yours at a scene of a murder," said Lucas.

"Yeah and what's that?" said David.

Lucas placed the wallet in front of him.

"That can't be, I've got my wallet right here," said David.

David took his wallet out of his trousers back pocket and showed it to them. When Lucas looked inside it, he could see it was almost identical to the one found at the crime scene Even the ID in the wallet looked the same. At this point, Lucas stepped outside and asked Jordan to step out too.

"What do you think, do you think he's being set up?" said Lucas.

"Yeah, I do. I felt that was the case before we went into the interview room," said Jordan.

"What makes you think that?"

"I don't have any evidence, it's just a gut feeling that I have."

"So, what do you suggest we do with David?"

"Well, you are able to hold him for twenty-four hours without charge. I would suggest you do that and release him tomorrow morning and see what happens," said Jordan.

What Jordan was planning was for Lucas to keep David overnight and to release him at nine o'clock in the morning. At that time, Jordan would be outside waiting for him. Then, she would follow him to see what he would do. At that, Jordan left the station and Carl took her and Jarvis back to the bed and breakfast. On the journey back, Jordan told Jarvis and Carl of the plan for the morning.

For the rest of the day Jordan relaxed. Jordan asked Hazel, the bed and breakfast owner, if she could have her breakfast at seven in the morning because she had to be out at a certain time.

Before she knew it, it was six o'clock in the morning and Jordan was getting herself ready for the day ahead. The first thing that she did when she was out of bed was to have a shower, then she got dressed. When she had just about finished getting dressed there was a knock on her door. When she opened it Jarvis was stood there. Jarvis told her that he would go with her while she followed David. They talked about how they would go about it, and it was decided that Jordan would follow David on foot and Jarvis wouldn't be too far away in the car.

By seven o'clock the two of them were in the dining room having their breakfasts. They didn't really speak much while they were eating, mainly because Jordan was thinking about following David and what he may do once he was released from the station. When they had finished their breakfasts they just sat there – Jordan sat there thinking and Jarvis sat there drinking his cup of coffee. After sitting there for about forty minutes or so Jordan decided that it was time to make their way to the station. It didn't take them too long to get there. When they arrived at the station Jordan parked the car at the side of the building away from the front doors. This was because when David would be released he would come through the front doors and she didn't want him to see her. When the time was almost a quarter to nine, Jordan's mobile started to ring. When she answered it, it was Lucas telling her that he was about to release David and he wondered if she was in position. When she said that she was, Lucas started the process of releasing David.

Jordan got out of the car and went to stand next to the police station, so that she could peer round the corner to the front doors. While she did so Jarvis got himself into the driver's seat. After about ten minutes of waiting, David came walking out of the front doors. For a moment or so he just stood there and looked around. As Jordan was peering round the station watching David, he looked in her direction and she darted backwards. Luckily for Jordan, David didn't see her.

When David started to walk away he was heading in Jordan's direction. When she peered round and saw him she got out of sight as quickly as she could. For a moment she couldn't find anywhere to hide. Then, she saw a public phone box and got to it as quickly as possible. When she was inside the phone box she pretended to make a phone call. Then, she looked to see where David was going. She could see David walking down the road and it appeared that he didn't notice her. When he was a little way away,

Jordan came out of the phone booth and started to follow David. Jarvis saw what was happening and he started to follow them, the best he could, in the car.

What Jordan didn't know was that Lucas had got some officers in plain clothes to follow David and to back up Jordan, if she needed it. Soon, they were heading away from the station. At first, Jordan assumed David would be going home to his caravan, but after a while she wasn't too sure. Jordan didn't know Cornwall that well but it appeared to her that he was going in a different direction, a direction that led away from the caravan park. Suddenly, David jumped on a bus and the bus set off. For a moment Jordan stood there and wondered what to do next. While she was standing there Jarvis pulled up beside her and she got in. When she was in the car Jarvis started to follow the bus.

While they were following the bus Jordan noticed some of the road signs and every one of them said St Ives on them. Jordan began to wonder why David was going to St Ives. Just before they entered St Ives the bus stopped and David got off. When Jordan saw this she asked Jarvis to pull over so that she could get out of the car. Just before she got out of the car she had a quick look to see which direction David was going. When he was off the bus David started to walk away from Jordan, so she got out of the car and followed him. Jarvis followed the best he could in the car. As Jordan, again, was following David on foot, the officers that Lucas had sent to back up Jordan had finally caught up with them.

After a while David went in what appeared to be a park area. It was a warm, sunny morning and there were several people in the park enjoying the warm weather. Jordan began to wonder why David had come here. David strolled over to sit on a bench. Jordan got herself behind a nearby tree so David couldn't see her but she could still watch him. While she was watching him David pulled out his mobile from his jacket pocket and looked at it. Then, he started to press the buttons on the phone as if he was writing and sending a text message. When he had finished he put the phone back in his pocket and started to look around as if he was waiting for someone.

After about five more minutes Jordan saw someone in the distance and they appeared to be walking in the direction of David. When the person had got to David and had sat down next to him, Jordan tried to move closer so she could listen to what they were saying. Jordan could see that the man who had joined David was a fair bit older. Soon, she was stood by a tree that was directly behind them and she could just about hear what they were saying. It appeared to her the two of them knew each other very well. At this point, Jordan began to wonder if the older man was David's father. All the time she was listening neither of them talked about the murders, but that was about to change.

"So, you've been questioned by the police over these murders, then?" said the older man.

"Yeah, but it's nothing to worry about," said David.

"Are you sure about that?"

"Of course, they don't have any evidence to say otherwise," said David.

When Jordan heard this, it convinced her that David must have something to do with these murders, but she wasn't sure what. After a few more minutes of sitting there talking the two stood up and went for a walk. Jordan let them get a little way ahead of her, then she started to follow them. The two men continued to talk while they walked, but Jordan wasn't close enough to hear what they were saying.

While she was following them something caught her eye to her right hand side. When she looked she could see that it was another man who appeared to have a particular interest in these two men as well. When this person saw her looking at him he went over to her. He explained that he was a police officer and he had been sent, with a few other officers, by Lucas just in case she needed any help. When Jordan looked back she couldn't see David or his companion. Then, in the distance she saw them walking towards the road. So, she hurried to catch up with them. As she caught up with them the two men reached the road, got into a car and drove away. By the time Jarvis had driven round to her position, the two men were already out of sight. While she was stood there the officer she was just talking to came and stood next to her.

"What do you think we should do now?" said the officer.

"Just let him go. We will not catch him now," said Jordan.

By now, the other officers that Lucas had sent had come over to see what was happening. Then, Jordan's mobile started to ring. When she answered it, it was Lucas. Jordan explained what had happened and that they would have to find another way to find out what David was up to. When Jordan and Lucas had finished talking she told the officers that Lucas wanted them back at the station and Jordan went back to the bed and breakfast with Jarvis.

As all this was going on, what they didn't realise was the killer had seen them following David. So he started to relax a bit more, although the voice said, "Don't relax too much, keep your mind on your work." As he heard the voice the killer started to play with a pocket watch that was in his jacket pocket and smiled.

CHAPTER EIGHT

N ow, it was late afternoon and the killer started to think where he could pitch his tent for the night. After watching Jordan and the police following David the killer was really content with himself.

The killer decided to go back to the wooded area he was the previous night. "Are you sure that you want to go back there. Remember, those two ramblers saw you there," said the voice. The voice had put a little bit of doubt in the killer's mind, so he went for a walk around the park while he decided on where to go. While he was walking he saw an empty bench. He was feeling a little tired with carrying all his things, so he went for a sit down. A little earlier in the day the killer had bought himself several bottles of water; he was feeling a little thirsty so he opened one of the bottles.

As he was drinking his bottle of water the killer was having a look around. There were still a few people in the park area enjoying the late afternoon sun. The killer thought that he had better make a move to find somewhere to pitch his tent for the night. As he was about to stand up someone caught his eye. It was a young woman in her early to mid-twenties with long light brown hair. She was wearing dark grey jogging trousers, a red T-shirt, training shoes and she was about five feet six inches tall. "That's the one, she your next victim. Go on," said the voice. The killer stood up and started to follow the woman.

While he was following the woman the killer had to carry all his things. After a little while he started to become quite tired, mainly because the woman was walking quite fast. The one thing he did notice while following the woman was that she was walking away from where it was most busy. Soon, there was no one else around, just the two of them.

Suddenly, the woman stopped, had a little look around on the ground and then she sat down. When she was comfortable, she had a look in a bag that she was carrying and pulled out a book to read. For a moment the killer just stood there and didn't know what to do. A little way to his left was another bench, so he went and sat on it while he decided what to do next. He kept an eye on the woman but also looking out in case anyone else might join them.

Just to the right of where the woman was sitting was quite a large bush. The killer thought the bush would be a good spot to hide his things while he dealt with the young woman. "Your things are safe, go and do what you need to do," said the voice. The killer stood at the side of the bush and peered round at the woman. When he saw that she was still reading he double checked there was no one else around and began to approach the woman. But as he was about to do the deed someone came along walking his dog. When the dog walker saw what was happening he shouted a warning to the woman.

For a moment both the killer and the woman froze. Then, the killer raced to the bush, grabbed his stuff and got out of the area as quickly as he could. The dog walker went across to the woman to make sure she was alright. When he had done that he pulled out his mobile phone and called the police. When he was through to the police he told them what had just happened and where he was. Lucas was told about this straight away and he made his way to the area. Before he left his desk Lucas gave Jordan a call and updated her.

Jordan and Jarvis were just arriving back at the bed and breakfast when she received the call. When she had finished talking to Lucas, Jarvis turned the car around and went back to the park.

When they arrived back at the park, there was a couple of police cars already there, so Jarvis parked behind one of them. Jordan couldn't see where the incident had taken place, but then she saw a police officer walking towards her. When Jordan approached the officer he recognised her and told her where Lucas was. Jordan and Jarvis made their way to Lucas's position as quickly as they could. Within a few minutes Jordan could see Lucas. She could see him talking to a young woman who was clearly upset. When Lucas saw Jordan, he finished talking to the woman and started to walk towards her.

"So, what's happened, then?" said Jordan.

"The young lady you've just seen me talking to was sat over there reading a book and whilst doing that she possibly came face to face with the killer," said Lucas.

"What about the guy with the dog, is he a witness?" said Jordan.

"Yeah, if it wasn't for him she could have been the next victim," said Lucas.

"How do you mean?"

"As the woman was about to be attacked, the dog walker saw what was happening and shouted a warning. When he shouted, the person that we've assumed to be the killer did a runner."

"So, he will be out of the area by now."

"I would imagine so, but you look a little puzzled about something."

"Yeah, when I was here earlier following David, this person who we've assumed to be the killer must have been in the park then," said Jordan.

"That's possible," said Lucas.

"What I'm going to do is to drive around the area. Because if this guy is on foot it could be possible that he hasn't got too far."

"Before I forget, the dog walker said that this guy ran off with some bags and that they looked really heavy."

At that, Jordan and Jarvis headed back to the car and Lucas made sure that he got the contact details from the young woman and the dog walker. While they were doing that the killer was still getting himself out of the area. He had decided to pitch his tent and camp out in the same area as the previous night. The killer knew that the police were probably looking for him, so he took the back streets to get out of the area. He knew they would be much quieter and there would be less chance of him being seen. As he was making his way to the wooded area to pitch his tent he kept looking around to see if there were any police.

"Don't forget that PI," said the voice.

Eventually the killer was on the road, the one that led to the wooded area. This road was a very long one and it was more open than all the rest he had walked along. So there was a better chance of him being seen by someone. While he was walking along the road he noticed a car driving slowly towards him. When he looked he saw that it was Jordan who was driving the car. As they passed each other both Jordan and the killer looked at one another. When Jordan looked at him and saw that he matched the description of the person that she was looking for she wanted to turn around as quickly as she could. As usual when she wanted to turn the car round quickly there was a whole line of traffic coming the other way.

As Jordan was trying to turn around the killer picked up his pace in the hope he was able to get to the wooded area. As the killer was getting closer to the wooded area Jordan was still trying to turn around. She couldn't believe how much traffic there was, but finally she got her chance. After she turned around she could just about see the killer in the distance. Jordan sped up to try and catch up with him. When she was about a hundred feet behind him the killer had reached the edge of the wooded area. The first chance he had he got himself within the trees and tried to find the perfect place to hide. Jordan saw this and she stopped the car at the point where he went into the woods.

Before she got out of the car Jordan asked Jarvis to call Lucas, tell him what was going on and to stay with the car and wait for Lucas. Then, Jordan got out of the car and went to look for the killer.

When Jordan reached the opening that the killer had gone through she paused for a moment. With her not knowing exactly where the killer was she was feeling a little nervous; she knew she was supposed to wait for back up but this was the closest she had been to the killer. Jordan knew that the killer needed to be caught, so she took a deep breath and then she went to look for him. As Jordan made her way into the trees she did so very carefully, her eyes were everywhere. She knew the killer could have hidden himself anywhere.

As Jordan made her way carefully through the trees, the killer was trying to put as much distance between himself and Jordan as he could. While he was making his way through the trees he was looking around to see if there was anywhere for him to hide. But despite searching, he couldn't find a suitable place. "Come on, you can't be caught now, find somewhere to hide," said the voice.

Jordan was still a fair way behind the killer but she suddenly caught sight of him. So, she sped up a little to try and catch up with him. At that point the killer turned around and saw her. "Look, she's following you. You need to do something," said the voice. While he was trying to get away from Jordan, the killer could hear cars travelling along a nearby road. Then, when he looked to his right he could see through the trees and saw a road in the distance. He knew that he probably wouldn't get away from Jordan by continuing to go through the trees, so he took the chance by going to the road. The killer knew that on the road he would have a chance of getting a taxi or jumping on a bus.

Jordan could see what he was doing and she wondered why he was heading towards the road. As they were quite close to the road the killer could see a bus pulling into its stop. He picked up his pace and tried to get on the bus before it pulled away. Now, Jordan could see what he was trying to do, so she picked up her pace to try and catch him. The killer managed to get to the bus before it pulled away, he got on the bus, paid his fare and sat down. Luckily for him, Jordan didn't get to the bus in time before it pulled away. At this, he gave a very big sigh of relief. Before the bus set off, Jordan saw that the bus was going to Land's End, but she didn't know exactly where. Jordan knew there was nothing else she could do here, so she went back to the car where Jarvis was waiting.

The killer knew Land's End quite well and he was sure he could find somewhere to hide out for a while. As he was sat there enjoying the ride the killer noticed a couple of people sat three seats in front of him and on the opposite side of the bus. He seemed to recognise them, then he remembered, they were the ramblers he had seen the previous day. As he was sat there he hoped that the two ramblers didn't spot him.

The ramblers had quite loud voices and the killer could hear them talking. The ramblers were talking about the murders and the killer could tell that the other passengers were listening. On the journey to Land's End they did nothing but talk about the murders, but the killer was just thankful that they didn't turn around and see him.

Before long the bus was arriving in Land's End. The killer didn't want to be seen by the ramblers, so he stayed in his seat until they were off the bus; he then got out of his seat and disembarked.

The killer got off the bus at Land's End. He knew the Land's End area well and he had two or three places in mind where he could hide out. Not too far from where he was there were some caves. Near these caves were some large rocks and boulders that he could hide amongst, so he headed over to them. The direction the killer was going was a totally different direction to the ramblers which he was grateful for. As he was walking the killer kept looking around to make sure he wasn't being followed by Jordan or the police.

While the killer was making his way to his potential hideout, Jordan was back at the car with Jarvis. When she arrived at the car Lucas was there and he was talking to Jarvis.

"I take it that you've lost him, then?" said Lucas.

"Yeah, he managed to get on a bus which set off before I got there," said Jordan.

"Any idea of where the bus was heading?" asked Lucas.

"Land's End."

The three of them talked for a little while longer, then, they went their separate ways. Before they went back to the bed and breakfast Jordan decided to have a drive to Land's End, on the off chance that they ran into the killer.

While in the car travelling to Land's End Jordan was very quiet. She was thinking that the killer always seemed to be one step ahead of her. Jarvis was driving, which gave Jordan the opportunity to have a real good look around for the killer. As she was sat in the passenger seat, her mind drifted to a case she had a few years earlier. It was a case of a serial killer who turned out to be really difficult to catch. Jordan remembered that the killer in that case suffered from a mental illness. What she was beginning to wonder was if the killer in the current case had any history with mental illness.

Before long they were arriving in Land's End. Jordan knew that the killer was probably here already and off the bus, so she started to look at every face in the hope that she would see the killer. After about twenty minutes of driving around Jordan asked Jarvis if he could park the car, because she wanted to have a walk around the areas where they couldn't drive.

When they had found a parking spot the two of them got out of the car and started to walk around. What the two of them didn't realise was that they were much closer to the killer than they might think. About half a mile from their position, there were the rocks that the killer was going to hide at and the two of them were walking straight towards them.

While the two of them were walking towards the rocks the killer was already there making himself comfortable. He was totally unaware that Jordan was only half a mile away.

The killer had found himself a perfect spot. He had managed to find a six feet by eight feet space between the rocks. When he had sat down he saw that he was surrounded by rocks, which made it very difficult for anyone to see him. When he looked up he saw that there was a rock that was overhanging. This overhang would make it more difficult for people to see him and it would protect him a little bit from any bad weather. The ground that he was sat on was soft, but was firm enough for him to pitch his tent, but he decided to leave that job until a little later.

While he was sat there the killer could hear people talking as they walked along a nearby path. Suddenly, he heard a voice that he recognised. When he listened more closely he could tell the voice belonged to Jordan. "She knows you're here, what are you going to do about it?" said the voice. For a moment or so he just sat there and listened. As he listened to her he could tell that she was stood still and she wasn't too far away from him, and he could hear her talking about him and the case.

"I wonder where he is?" said Jordan.

"He could be anywhere in Land's End," said Jarvis.

"Yeah, but I can't help but feel that he is somewhere close," said Jordan.

Just then, a police car and an ambulance went past them very quickly with their lights and sirens on. While they were watching them Jordan received a phone call.

"Hello," said Jordan.

"Where are you?" said Lucas.

"We're in Land's End," said Jordan.

"There's been an incident in Land's End and it could be connected to our case," said Lucas.

"Yeah, whereabouts?"

Lucas told Jordan where the incident had taken place and gave her directions on how to get there. When Jordan knew where she was going both she and Jarvis made their way back to the car as quickly as they could. As they did so Jordan told Jarvis what was happening. Unbeknown to them they only had been a few feet away from the killer and he was so relieved that they had moved away from the area.

When they were in the car Jordan followed the directions that Lucas had given her and soon they were arriving at the place of the incident. Before they got out of the car Jordan had a look around the scene. What she saw were a couple of paramedics attending to a young woman, two police officers taking statements and a small crowd that had gathered. For a moment or so Jordan sat there and tried to work out what had happened. While she was sat there she saw Lucas walking towards her, so she got out of the car to talk to him.

"So, what's happened here?" said Jordan.

"This young lady being treated by the paramedics has been attacked. From the way she was attacked it would suggest that she was attacked by the person we're looking for," said Lucas.

"I'm wondering why he didn't finish the job?" said Jordan.

"Because he was interrupted and the ones who did the interrupting are giving their statements to the uniformed officers," said Lucas.

At that, Jordan had a look around the scene from where she was stood. She started by watching the paramedics treat the victim. When the victim was ready she was taken to the ambulance and then off to hospital. Then Jordan looked at the small crowd that had gathered and she saw a face that she recognised: David Crammer.

"Take a look at who is at the crime scene," said Jordan.

"Who am I looking at?" said Lucas.

"David Crammer, he is over there in the small crowd."

"Yes, I see him."

At that, both Jordan and Lucas started to walk towards David. When David saw them walking towards him he started to walk away. Before they knew it David set off running; when Jordan saw this she set off after him. The two officers that were taking statements had finished so Lucas told them to back up Jordan and chase after David. As the two of them started to chase David, Jordan was beginning to catch up with him. Then, David ran into a crowded arcade with Jordan following closely behind. The further they went into the arcade the more crowded it seemed to be. Suddenly Jordan lost sight of David in the crowds. She stopped running and had a real good look around to see if she could see him. The two officers that Lucas had sent to help Jordan had caught up and were also looking round for David.

David had found an empty room to hide in. The room appeared to be some kind of office and David was lucky that there was no one in the office. From where David was hiding he could see Jordan and the two officers looking for him. For a brief moment Jordan glanced in his direction, so he ducked down behind a filing cabinet hoping that she didn't see him. After a few seconds David looked over the filing cabinet. When he did so, he could see Jordan and the officers beginning to walk away. There were a couple of ways out of the arcade and David knew where they were. So, David watched the three of them walk away. When he thought it was safe for him to do so he came out of his hiding place and made his way to the exit in the opposite direction.

When he was out of the arcade David made his way out of the area as quickly as he could. He knew that Jordan and the police would go to his caravan to look for him, so he had to decide if he should take a chance on going back there.

CHAPTER NINE

—

A s Jordan made her way back to the scene after chasing David, she was wondering why he'd been at the scene and why had he run when she and Lucas went to talk to him. The only logical reason she could think of was that he was involved in the case somehow or he knew more about these murders then he was telling the police.

While she was making her way back to the scene she suddenly got the feeling that she was being followed. When she looked around she saw that the only people that were close to her were the two officers who'd helped her chase David. Every time she got this feeling that she was being followed she was usually right. One of the officers saw that Jordan was looking a little puzzled, so he went across to her to see if he could be of any assistance.

"Is there anything the matter, Miss Lewis?" said the officer.

"Yes, I think that we're being followed. So, without making it too obvious could you and the other officer drop back a touch and have a look to see if I'm right," said Jordan.

So, the officer did what Jordan asked. The officer told his colleague what she wanted him to do. The officers slowed down a little, as did Jordan. After almost a minute Jordan was sure that there was someone to her right but behind her slightly. This person seemed to be getting closer to her with every passing moment. When the person was about a foot or two from her Jordan turned and challenged them.

"Who are you?" said Jordan.

"I'm Mark Barker, I'm a local journalist and you are Jordan Lewis?" said the person.

"Yes I am, but why are you following me?"

"Because I'm working on a story about the pocket watch killer and I was wondering if you had anything to say about it," said Mark.

"How do you know that I'm not in Cornwall on holiday?"

"Because my sources tell me that you are a private investigator that is working on the case. Plus, I've just watched you chase David Crammer with the two officers that are stood just behind you."

"In that case you will know that I can't talk about an active investigation."

"Do you think David is involved in the case somehow?"

"I can't say either way. But what do you think?"

"Well, I've been watching David for a little while and he certainly seems to be up to something," said Mark.

"While you've been watching David have you seen anyone else with him?" said Jordan.

"I can't think of anyone. But you know when I come to think of it, there was one time when I followed David to a local cemetery. When he arrived there he met with a guy and they talked for a while. Another time I followed David to his home on the caravan park and I saw the same guy. It looked like he lived in the caravan opposite David's."

"Could you tell me what this guy looked like?"

Mark went on to describe the other person. As Mark spoke Jordan listened very carefully. The more she heard the more she realised that the other person she had encountered a few times, the one she thought could be the killer. Jordan didn't tell Mark that she and the police felt that the other person that Mark had seen was the lead suspect in the case. This was because in Jordan's experience if the press are given too much information they sometimes have the habit of getting in the way of cases by letting slip too much information to the public. This information could find itself in the hands of a suspect which would help him avoid arrest. But sometimes on a case Jordan likes to keep in touch with local reporters because they can be a good source of information. So, before she went back to the scene she exchanged business cards with Mark so that she could keep up to date with that information.

Meanwhile, the killer was still at his hideout amongst the rocks on the beach. Now it was late afternoon and he could see that the tide was beginning to come in. For the time being he relaxed and the voice was silent. Even though it was late afternoon he could still hear people walking by on the path that was above his head. He could even tell that some of the people had a dog with them.

Then, his stomach started to rumble and he began to feel hungry. He realised that he was just in the mood for some fish and chips. He had some money with him and there was a fish and chip shop not too far from where he was. He didn't want to take his things with him, so he decided to leave them where they were until he got back, but he made sure they were well hidden. When he had done that he waited until it was quiet. When he couldn't hear anyone walking up and down the path above, he started to come slowly out of his hiding place.

He could see that there wasn't anyone close to him so at this point, he very quickly went to get his fish and chips. On his way to the shop he maintained his vigilance. He looked around because he didn't want to be seen by the police. When he walked into the shop he could see that there were four people already in there waiting to be served. While he waited for his turn he tried to avoid eye contact with anyone.

He could hear the other customers talking. At first, he didn't pay much attention but then he realised what they were talking about. When he listened more closely he realised that they were talking about the murders. When he glanced around he saw that one of the customers was looking at him quizzically. This person had a newspaper in his hands. She looked down at the paper then back up at him. By now, the woman's order was ready so she took it off the staff member and walked out of the shop.

While the killer was watching the woman walk away, through the shop window he could see her walking towards his hiding place. He became aware of someone talking to him. When he turned around someone behind the counter was asking him what he wanted. So, he very quickly asked for fish and chips.

When he had his fish and chips and had paid for them he made his way out of the shop and began to look for the woman, but he couldn't see her anywhere. However, when he was getting close to his hiding place he could see someone near it. But luckily for the killer that person soon started to walk away. He crossed the road and made his way to his hideout. At this point, he heard the voice telling him to be more careful.

Soon, he was back at his hideout and was very well hidden by the rocks. He could see that his things were still where he had left them. While the killer was enjoying his fish and chips, Carl Benson, Jarvis's friend, was sat at home thinking about the case. After about two hours of sitting there he decided to go out and do something to help, but he didn't bother to tell anyone. He knew that Jordan and the police had found a barn that the killer had used and Carl knew where to find it. So, he went to have a look at it for himself. He put on his coat and shoes and was soon in his car.

On his journey to the barn Carl was wondering what he may find. Carl knew that Jordan and the police had searched the barn, but he wondered if they had missed anything. The first thing that he noticed was that he couldn't drive down to the barn, as the dirt path was too narrow for his car. So, he parked his car as far off the road as he could. When he had parked his car he noticed the police car that was parked there. It belonged to the officers that Lucas had left there to watch the barn, just in case the killer returned.

For a moment or so he just sat there. He was wondering what he would find when he arrived at the barn. He knew that he wouldn't discover anything by just sitting there, so he got out of his car, locked it and started to make his way towards the barn.

When Carl was at the entrance to the path he stood there for a moment and looked down the path. He saw that the path was quite narrow with trees on both sides. Carl was really curious about the barn and he started to make his way down the path. When he was only a few feet down the path Carl began to get an uncomfortable feeling. It was the kind of feeling that he was being watched. He looked from side to side to see if he could see anyone through the trees, but he couldn't. When he was a little further down the path he heard a snapping sound as if someone had stood on a twig, but when he looked in the direction where the sound had come from he couldn't see anything so he put the sound down to some kind of animal and he carried on down the path.

Soon, he was at the other end of the path and the barn came into view. Next, he saw the two officers that were watching the barn, just in case the killer came back. The officers recognised Carl straight away because of the cases he had helped Lucas with. Carl explained why he was there, then, he started to have a look around. As Carl got to the barn he could hear the two officers talking. When he turned around he could see that one of them was on his radio. As he watched them the two officers started to leave. Carl assumed they were going back to the station.

When Carl had watched the officers leave his attention reverted back to the barn. When he went over to the doors of the barn and tried to open them he realised that they were locked. So, he made his way round the side of the barn to see if there was another way in. As he was making his way to the back of the barn Carl was sure that he could hear something. At first, it sounded to Carl to be a small animal rustling through the nearby long grass.

When he was at the back of the barn Carl saw that there wasn't a door, but he did notice the window. When he was at the window he wondered if it was unlocked. He noticed that it was the type of window that slid to one side when it was open. When he tried moving it he realised that it was unlocked. From where he was stood he couldn't really see too much, so he climbed through the window so he could have a look around. With him being in his late fifties he struggled to climb through the window but he nevertheless managed it.

Once Carl was inside he had a slow walk around to see what he could discover. Before he walked anywhere Carl could tell that the killer didn't live in the barn, mainly because there wasn't a bed. As Carl started to walk around he could see that there were a lot of boxes everywhere. He also saw a fair bit of tinned food stacked up around the place. Just then, he heard something behind him. As he turned around he saw a shape go past the window. Carl was sure the shape he saw was a person. Now, he was feeling a little unnerved. Carl was so unnerved he decided to give Jordan a call.

"Hello," said Jordan.

"Hello Jordan, it's Carl. I was wondering if you had the time to come and help me," said Carl in a whisper.

"Why are you whispering?"

"Because I am inside the barn that we believe is used by the killer and I'm sure that someone is walking around outside."

"That is probably the two officers that Lucas had left there to watch the barn."

"It can't be, they have already left," said Carl.

"Okay, we will make our way there," said Jordan.

Jordan and Jarvis had been on their way back to the bed and breakfast, so they changed direction to head to the barn. While he waited for them to arrive, Carl stayed away from the window. Also, he looked for somewhere to hide just in case whoever was outside looked through the window. As he very quickly looked around he saw some boxes stacked up quite high, so he went and hid behind them. When he was behind the boxes he crouched to make sure that he couldn't be seen by anyone who would look through the window. While he was crouched down his mind began to race. He began to wonder if the killer had come back now that the police had left.

While he was crouched behind the boxes Carl was sure he could hear someone walking along one side of the barn. He knew that it couldn't be Jordan because she couldn't have got to the barn in such a short period of time; from what Carl could hear it sounded like whoever it was they were walking from the back of the barn to the front. In Carl's mind the only person it could be was the killer. Then, Carl heard something at the front of the barn. In front of where he was there was a work bench of some sort, but he was still able to see the top section of the barn doors. For a moment Carl didn't hear anything, but then he saw the barn doors move as if someone was checking if they were unlocked. At this point, as far as Carl was concerned, Jordan couldn't get to the barn quickly enough.

By now, Jordan and Jarvis were only two miles from the barn. They couldn't understand what Carl was doing at the barn in the first place. Jordan was also wondering if the two officers that Lucas had left at the barn had been pulled away, who was it that Carl could hear walking around. The only person she could possibly think it might be was the killer. Jordan knew the killer only killed women, but she knew if he found Carl at the barn he could make an exception in his case, so she drove the last couple of miles as quickly as she could.

Back at the barn Carl was really beginning to panic. This was because whoever was outside was really trying to get in. Then, Carl was certain he could hear whoever it was at the back of the barn and they seemed to be near the window. Carl decided to peer over the boxes he was hiding behind, but he suddenly saw the shape of a person appear at the window and he ducked back down again. From the glimpse that Carl got of the person he could tell that it wasn't Jordan or Jarvis. He started to think to himself if it wasn't them then who was it? As he was crouched behind the boxes he could hear the window opening and someone climbing through the window into the barn. Now, Carl was really beginning to pray for Jordan to hurry up and get there. He could now hear footsteps slowly making their way in his direction.

Carl then noticed a wall mirror. The mirror was at floor level, stood on one edge and leaning against some boxes. It was in just the right position so that Carl could see behind him towards the window. What he could see, among all the items in the barn, was someone walking slowly towards him. As the person got a little closer to him

Carl could see the person wearing a hooded sweatshirt with the hood over his head covering most of his face. Then, when the person was about four or five feet behind him, voices could be heard from outside and the person stopped in his tracks. When Carl listened more closely, he could tell they were the voices of Jordan and Jarvis.

When the person heard the voices he turned back towards the window and made his way out of the barn as quickly as he could. When he got to the window he started to climb out as Jordan and Jarvis were about halfway along the barn on the right hand side. When the person had climbed out of the window he ran as fast as he could away from the barn and towards the left. When the two of them were at the back of the barn the person was out of sight. When they were at the window Jordan called out to Carl. When he heard Jordan's voice, Carl came out of his hiding place and made his way to the window.

"So, where's this person, then?" said Jordan.

"He just ran off when he heard the two of you talking," said Carl.

"He was actually in the barn and he didn't see you?" said Jordan.

"No he didn't, but I was hiding," said Carl.

Carl slowly climbed out of the window. When he was outside the barn, the three of them made their way to Jordan's car. The stranger was hiding behind a tree not too far away and he watched the three of them walk away.

While the three of them made their way to Jordan's car, Lucas was sat at his desk thinking about the case. As he was sat there he began to wonder if Mandy, the pathologist, had found anything of interest in the autopsy of the most recent victim. He reached for the phone to give her a ring but then decided to drive round and see her.

While he was making his way down to his car Lucas started to think about the killer. He wondered where he was and what he was doing. Lucas couldn't help but feel that the killer was close and he would probably hear from him soon enough. But what Lucas didn't realise was that he would hear from the killer much sooner than anyone would dare think.

Lucas was soon in his car and driving round to the morgue. As he drove to the morgue he deliberately took his time. This was because he wanted to have a look around on the off chance he spotted the killer. He had an idea of what the killer looked like because of when the killer left the pocket watch in the reception area of the station, when he was caught on the security camera.

While Lucas was making his way to the morgue the killer was still in his hideout. He had finished his fish and chips and he was looking out to sea. While he was sat there the voice started to talk to him. "You can't just sit here, you need to get back to work," said the voice. The killer tried to ignore the voice but the voice went on and on and wouldn't stop.

In an attempt to block out the voice the killer decided to go for a walk. He made sure that his things were tucked away and well hidden, then, he set off for a walk. He didn't want to go too far really so he started by going for a walk along the beach. With it being late afternoon it was becoming a little cooler. When he felt the chill in the air the killer fastened his coat up a little more. "What do you think you are doing, you don't have the time to go for a nice little stroll on the beach," said the voice. But the killer just carried on walking. After about half an hour the tide was a fair way in. So, the killer decided to go elsewhere for a walk.

The killer decided to go to the area where most of the shops were and do a little window shopping. As he turned a corner of a street where several shops were he suddenly went off the idea of window shopping. This was because a little over twenty feet in front of him was someone that he recognised. It was the woman from the fish and chip shop, the one who had kept on looking at him. "She's the one, she's your next victim," said the voice. Luckily for the killer the woman had her back to him. "Go on, you know you want to," said the voice. The woman started to walk away, so the killer began to follow.

As he was following the woman, the killer kept looking around, because he didn't want to be seen by the police. Every so often the woman would stop and look in a window. When the killer saw this he stopped and pretended to look in a window. As he was stood there he had another look around to check for police. Then, the woman started to walk off again.

Soon, the woman was walking away from the area that had the shops. What she didn't realise was that she was being followed. At the moment she was in two minds. She was deciding to rather go back home or to stay out and get more fresh air. While she decided she walked in the general direction of her home. The one thing the killer noticed while they were walking was that they were heading into a much quieter area. Now being in a quieter area the killer was getting ready to make his move. He picked up his pace a little to get closer to the woman, looking everywhere to make sure that no one else was around. As the killer was about to make his move, the woman bumped into one of her friends and they started talking. At this point, the killer was so close to the woman the only thing he could do was to carry on walking past them.

When the killer had walked past them, he found himself a vantage point so he could watch them without being noticed. About ten to twelve feet past the women was a low wall and he sat on it. From where he was sat he could just about see the two of them and it wasn't obvious that he was watching them. While he was sat there he heard a car travelling towards him from his left. As he looked the car drove past, but he also noticed a police car parked about halfway down the road. "Look, the police. You are going to have to be careful," said the voice.

While the killer watched the police car with interest, to see if it moved, the woman finished talking with her friend and started walking away. At first, the killer didn't notice the woman walking away because he was so interested in watching the police car. But when he turned back around he saw that the woman had moved away. For a frantic few seconds he looked around to see if he could see where she had gone. Then, he saw her a little way down the street. "Come on now, keep your mind on the game," said the voice.

The killer gave the police car one last look, then he started to follow the woman again. This time while following the woman he was really conscious about the police. Seeing the police car really unnerved him a fair bit. He was beginning to think about calling it a day and going back to his hideout. "You can't stop now, you've a job to finish," said the voice. At this point, the killer really didn't know what to do for the best. While he was following the woman and trying to work out what he should do, he could hear a car coming up behind him. When he glanced over his shoulder he saw that it was the police car that he had noticed a couple of minutes ago. "Calm down, they don't know who you are," said the voice. The killer put his head down and didn't make eye contact with the officers in the car. The police car slowly drove by, but for one brief moment the car seemed to pause just by the killer. For that moment the killer's heart seemed to stop, but he breathed a sigh of relief as the car drove by. He watched as the car turned left a little further ahead. "That was a little close for comfort, but you can get on with things now," said the voice.

He didn't get too close to the woman for the time being – this was because he wanted to make sure the police car wasn't coming back. After a few minutes and no sign of the police car, the killer was as confident as he could be that the police car wasn't coming back. Now, the killer's attention was back on the woman. They were on a street which had houses on both sides While they were walking he could see the woman was getting some keys out of her jeans pocket. "Those look like house keys. We must be near her home, you have to do something," said the voice. Just then the woman turned right and started to walk up a path to a house. "Quick, you need to do something," said the voice. The killer quickly followed the woman up the path, pushed her in as she opened the door and then followed her in, closing the door behind them. The woman turned around all shocked and stunned. When she looked at the killer she recognised him from the fish and chip shop.

"You're the pocket watch killer that's all over the news, aren't you? I thought it may have been you in the chippy," said the woman.

The killer just stood there in silence. Behind the woman he could see the kitchen. He forced the woman into the kitchen and made her sit at the kitchen table. "Ask her if she lives alone," said the voice.

"Do you live alone?" asked the killer.

"Yes," said the woman.

While she was sat at the table the killer started to look through the cupboards and drawers. He was looking for something to tie up the woman with. Eventually he found some string that he could use. He tied her up to the chair and used a tea towel as a gag.

When he had finished and was happy the woman wouldn't be able to get out of the chair, he walked back into the hall. "She knows who you are, she knows what you look like, you need to do something," said the voice. Now, the killer was becoming really worked up, he began to pace up and down the hallway. This was the first time that he had been in a potential victim's home. "What if someone comes to the house?" he thought to himself.

While the killer was deciding what to do with the woman, Lucas was arriving at the morgue. When he found a parking spot and had parked his car he made his way in to see Mandy. But there was no sign of Mandy at her office, so he went to have a look to see if she was conducting an autopsy. As he was making his way to the autopsy room, he started to feel a little unsettled. He put the feeling down to him not liking being around dead bodies. Then, he heard a clanking sound but he couldn't tell where it was coming from. Just then, he heard a voice coming from just behind him and he nearly jumped out of his skin.

"A little jumpy today, aren't we?" said Mandy.

"It's being around dead bodies, I can never get used to it," said Lucas.

"Is there anything that I can do for you?"

"Yes, I was wondering if you had done the autopsy on the most recent victim yet?"

"Yes I have. My report is in my office."

"Is there anything that you can tell me?"

"Basically the same as the others, same cause of death, no fingerprints, no DNA no nothing. Everything just the same," said Mandy.

By now, the two of them were back in Mandy's office. Mandy handed her report to Lucas and the two of them sat down at Mandy's desk. Lucas had a quick glance through the report, then he put the report on the edge of Mandy's desk and sat back in his chair.

"Sometimes I think that we'll never catch this guy," said Lucas.

"He will make a mistake sooner or later, they all do," said Mandy.

Just then, Lucas's mobile phone started to ring. When he answered his phone it was the station, they informed Lucas that there had been a possible sighting of the killer. Lucas wrote down the location as it was given to him. He briefly told Mandy what was happening then he raced out to his car. Lucas was really hoping that this was the break in the case that he was looking for. Soon, he was in his car driving to the location of the possible sighting. While he was driving he was wondering if this was the killer's mistake that Mandy was referring to.

Before long Lucas was arriving at the given location. It was a street with houses on both sides. There was already a marked police car at the scene. Lucas noticed that there was an officer already taking a statement. When Lucas had parked his car he got out and went to stand by the officer who was taking the statement. Soon, the officer was finished with the witness.

"So, what do we have, then?" said Lucas.

"The person I was just talking to was sure that she saw something a little strange about an hour ago," said the officer.

"What do you mean, a little strange?"

"She saw her neighbour across the street there arrive home and she was sure that her neighbour was bundled inside by a man."

"Did the witness say if she had seen the man before?"

"She hasn't personally seen the man before, but she is sure that she recognises him from the posters that have been put out. You know the ones, sir, the ones with the photo of the man in the station's reception area."

"Yes, I remember."

While they were talking, another police car with two officers inside pulled up. Lucas filled them in on what was happening and then sent them behind the house in question. This was because if the man used the back door to make his escape then they could grab him. While all this was going on the killer realised that there was something going on outside. The killer went into the living room to look through the window to see what was happening. Straight away he recognised Lucas. "See, they have found you. I knew this would happen," said the voice. The first thing the killer did was to get away from the window so he wouldn't be seen, but he was still close enough so he could see what was happening. "Think quickly, do something," said the voice. While he was thinking of what to do, Lucas and the other officer started to cross the road. Now, the killer was really becoming concerned. Then, his concern turned into curiosity. This was because Lucas had gone next door. The killer noticed that the living room window was open slightly. So, he took a chance and went a little closer so he could hear what was being said. But he stood next to the curtain so he would be hidden from Lucas.

While he was stood there he heard the door open and Lucas started to talk. From what he could hear a neighbour across the street had seen the woman being bundled into her house by someone and it was reported to the police. The woman explained that it was her new boyfriend messing around. As the woman was talking, her boyfriend came to the door and he confirmed her story. Lucas was satisfied with what he was told, but he did remind the couple about the serial killer that was in Cornwall and suggested for them to be careful in the future. Lucas left it at that and went back across the street with the officer. He then got on to the radio and told the other officers at the back of the house that it was all clear and for them to come back round to the front. When they were back round at the front the four of them had a chat for a minute or so then left the area. As the killer watched them leave he suddenly became more relaxed.

CHAPTER TEN

—

M ark Barker, the journalist, was sat in his car driving around. He had finished work for the day but he wasn't ready to go home just yet. So, he was having a drive around on the off chance he could get some kind of lead on his story, the one about the pocket watch killer.

On his passenger seat Mark had a copy of the poster that the police had handed out. The photo on the poster was the person who was in the police station's reception area, the one Lucas suspected was the killer. Mark was driving around in the hope that he got a glimpse of the killer. While Mark was at the set of traffic lights waiting for them to turn green, two police cars and a police van raced in front of him going from left to right with their lights and sirens blaring. As they went by the traffic lights changed to green, so out of professional curiosity Mark followed them to see what was happening. The police vehicles didn't travel too far past the traffic lights. About a quarter of a mile past the lights the police had stopped outside a house. The house that the police had stopped at was the house the killer had held the woman captive, but by now the killer was long gone.

Mark didn't park too close because he didn't want to get in the way of the police doing their jobs, but he was nevertheless close enough to see what was happening. While he was watching, the police made the scene secure. Then, within moments of each other, Lucas, Mandy the pathologist and Jane Brown the CSI all arrived at the scene. Mandy and Jane went straight in but Lucas stood on the pavement outside and looked around. He realised that he had been on this particular street a little earlier and had been next door. Lucas thought to himself if this was the work of the killer had he actually been here and in the house whilst he was next door. After another moment or so Lucas went inside the house.

As Lucas walked through the door and entered the house his eyes were everywhere. The main thing he was looking for was a pocket watch. If he found one that would confirm that this was the work of the pocket watch killer. He slowly walked down the hall and into the kitchen. When he was in the kitchen he immediately saw a young woman gagged and bound to a chair. Mandy and Jane were knelt down next to the body. Jane wanted the gag and string that the victim was tied up with as evidence. So, it was very slowly and very carefully removed from the victim and put into evidence bags. When this was done Mandy took care of the body and Jane looked around the kitchen for any other evidence.

While Mandy and Jane were doing their jobs, Lucas had a look around the kitchen from where he was stood. He was looking for a pocket watch, but he couldn't see one. So, he went to have a look around the rest of the house on the off chance that it had been left elsewhere.

He went back down the hallway a little way and into the living room. The living room seemed comfortably furnished with a nice looking sofa and matching armchairs, there was a rug on the varnished floorboards, a nice side unit, an expensive looking TV in one corner and a couple of paintings on the walls. When he'd had a real good look around the living room and couldn't see a pocket watch he went to have a look upstairs. But just as he was about to go upstairs he was called back into the kitchen. When Lucas was back in the doorway to the kitchen he could see that the victim was now laid out flat on the floor with Mandy and Jane paying particular attention to one pocket on the victim's trousers. With one gloved hand Jane pulled something out of the trouser pocket. As she pulled out the item everyone could see that it was a pocket watch.

"So, this was the work of the pocket watch killer, then," said Lucas.

At that point, Mandy put the body into a body bag in readiness to take it to the morgue and Jane continued to look for evidence. When Mandy was ready, her assistant took the body to the van. Lucas followed them and sat outside on the low wall in front of the house and gave Jordan a call. When she answered her phone, Lucas told her about the latest body that had been found. By now, Mark had got out of his car and had walked a little closer to the house. He saw the body come out of the house and the first thing he thought of was whether the body had anything to do with the pocket watch killer. Then, he saw Lucas sat on the wall and talking on the phone. Mark was interested to know what Lucas was talking about, so, he got a little closer to see if he could hear what he was saying.

He could tell that Lucas was talking about why he was at the house. Then, Mark heard Lucas say that a pocket watch had been found. Instantly this told Mark that he'd done the right thing by following the police cars in the first place. Now, he was going to hang around to see what information he could glean.

After Lucas had finished talking to Jordan on the phone he stayed at the house for a while as Jordan had said she would make her way to the house for a look herself, plus he wanted to see if Jane had found anything of interest.

By now, there was a crowd beginning to assemble. As Lucas waited for Jordan to arrive he looked around the crowd. It never ceased to amaze Lucas how someone's death brings out people's morbid curiosity. While he was looking at the crowd he saw a face that seemed familiar. He was sure that this person was the one who had left the pocket watch in the reception area of the station. To be sure Lucas went to have a look at the poster in his car. When he was in his car and looking at the poster he was certain that the person on the poster and the person in the crowd were one and the same. He returned to the small crowd and got a real good look at every face. While he was looking at the crowd he became aware of someone talking to him. When he turned around he saw that it was Jordan. She could tell that he was deep in thought about something.

"Is there something wrong?" asked Jordan.

"Yeah, I'm sure that the person on this poster was just in this crowd," said Lucas.

"He couldn't have got too far, we can go and have a look for him."

"Isn't Jarvis or Carl with you?"

"No, they are back at the bed and breakfast having a chat about the case."

At that, the two of them went to look for the person that Lucas had seen. Jordan had a quick look at the photo on the poster to remind herself who she was looking for. Now, Jordan's eyes were everywhere in the hope that she would catch a glimpse of this person. The person that Lucas had seen was actually the killer. The killer wasn't too far away and he was watching the two of them look for him. The killer didn't want to take any chances on them finding him, so he made his way to his hideout as quickly as he could. He went the quickest route he knew and his eyes were everywhere. Before long he was back among the rocks making himself as invisible as possible. He saw that his things were still there which was a relief to him. For the next few minutes he just sat there and relaxed.

By now, it was beginning to get dark. The killer prepared his sleeping bag and started to get himself comfortable for the night. While he was doing that Jordan and Lucas were still walking from street to street looking for the person Lucas had spotted among the small crowd. But by now, the two of them had begun to realise that the person they were looking for had almost certainly got away. So, they made their way back to the crime scene.

"Are you sure the person that you saw at the scene is the person that's on the poster?" said Jordan.

"Yes, I'm positive," said Lucas.

"Well, serial killers are known to come back to the scene of their crimes in an attempt to relive the crime," said Jordan.

Soon, the two of them were back at the scene. As they were about to go into the house, Jane came walking out. She told Lucas that, as well as the pocket watch, they had a couple of real good pieces of fingerprint evidence and she would update him on the outcome.

After Jane left, Lucas took Jordan into the house. Whenever possible Jordan liked to have a look around a crime scene, to give her a clearer and better picture in her head of the crime scene. The first place that Lucas took her was the kitchen. He explained that was where the woman's body had been found. Jordan wanted to know how she was found and what position she was in. When Jordan had been in the kitchen for a little while she went for a look around the rest of the house. Jordan wanted to see if she could find out how the victim lived her life. For this the house usually gives her a few clues. From the kitchen she went into the living room. When she walked through the door she could see the room was comfortably furnished. From the photos Jordan could tell that there probably wasn't a special someone in her life – the photos she could see only had the dead woman in them with an elderly couple, who Jordan assumed to be the woman's parents. On one wall there were a couple of shelves with seven trophies on them, two were for karate and five were for judo. This told Jordan that the victim was able to defend herself, but sadly not on this occasion. It told Jordan that the killer was very clever at gaining his victim's trust. Jordan walked around the rest of the house to see if she could get any more information. After a little while of walking round the house Jordan had got all the information she could get out of the house and she went back downstairs. Jordan noticed Lucas was in the living room talking to a man and woman. She didn't want to disturb them so she stayed in the hall. But when Lucas noticed Jordan he came out to talk to her.

"Who's that?" asked Jordan.

"They are the victim's parents. They didn't know that their daughter was dead and they've just come around for visit."

"To turn up like that out of the blue, it must have been a shock to them. How are they taking it?"

"Much better than I thought, I don't think it's fully hit them yet. Do you want to have a chat with them yet?"

"No thanks, I'm no good with grieving parents. I will get back to the bed and breakfast."

At that, Jordan left the house and made her way back to her car, where she just sat for a little while, thinking about the latest victim. Assuming that this was the work of the pocket watch killer – with a pocket watch being found at the scene there was nothing wrong in assuming that – then, this was the first time that the killer has been inside someone's home. While she was sat there Jordan saw Lucas come out of the house, get in his car and drive away. She assumed that he must have left the victim's parents to look after the house.

Jordan wasn't in the mood to go back to the bed and breakfast, so she went for a drive around, on the off chance she saw the killer. She began to wonder about David Crammer, the ex-con. She couldn't help but think that he had a connection of some kind to the case. Then, for some strange reason she had an urge to go to the caravan park. Even though she had chased David the day before, she knew that he would have to go back home sooner or later.

Soon, Jordan was arriving at the caravan park. She found a parking space just outside and walked on. Jordan knew which was David's static caravan and she went directly to it. She looked through one of the windows and she saw that the lights were turned off. When she tried the door she could tell that it was locked. Then, she went up to one of the windows and looked through to see if she could see anyone, but there was no one there. Jordan stood there for a moment and tried to think. She had a good feeling that sooner or later David would return home, so she decided to hang around for a while and wait for him to return. About twenty feet away there was a bench, so she went across to it and sat down. She made herself comfortable and waited for a while.

While Jordan was sat there waiting she noticed that in the static caravan opposite David's the light kept going on and off. At first, Jordan didn't think anything of it. But then, it began to dawn on her that the caravan opposite David's belonged to the killer. Now, Jordan was really curious so she went to investigate, although she was a little nervous being on her own.

As Jordan was slowly walking towards the caravan the light went off again and the door opened slightly. Jordan stopped in her tracks. She had a quick look around to see where she could hide. To her right there was another caravan, so she went and stood at the end of it. She then peered round the side of it to see who came out of the killer's caravan. Jordan could see that they were dressed in black with black training shoes, black trousers and a black hooded sweatshirt with the hood over their head. They stood outside the caravan for a moment and Jordan tried looking at their face, but she couldn't quite see. The person then closed the caravan door, locked it and started to walk away. Jordan was really curious to know who this person was so she started to follow them. She knew that she wanted to be at the caravan park for when David returned home, but she thought that finding out who this person was to be more important at this stage.

While she was following the person Jordan felt that she would be more comfortable with a little back up, so she gave Lucas a call. When Lucas answered his phone Jordan told him where she was, explained what was happening and that she could do with a little back up, just in case things went wrong for her. Lucas was on his way home but he told her that he would help her out. Lucas turned his car around when he was able to and went to back up Jordan.

It seemed to Jordan that the stranger was oblivious to her following them. Jordan was beginning to wonder who exactly the stranger really was. She was trying to work out what connection, if any, the stranger had with the case. The one thing Jordan did know with some degree of certainty was that the stranger must have some connection with the main suspect in the case. Jordan felt this because the stranger was in the killer's static caravan.

About half a mile away from the caravan park the stranger turned a corner, looking over their shoulder as they did so and looked directly at Jordan. She thought that the stranger had a manly face. Straight away Jordan knew that her cover was blown, so she got to where the stranger had turned as quickly as she could. But on reaching there she couldn't see the stranger anywhere. When she looked down the road she could see plenty of hiding places but no buildings. A few hundred yards in front of her Jordan could see that the road she had turned onto connected with another road, but she knew the stranger couldn't have gone that far.

As Jordan walked slowly down the road looking for the stranger she could see that there were plenty of hiding places. There were thick, tall bushes all along the road on both sides and the stranger could be anywhere behind them. Jordan knew the stranger was somewhere and she wasn't going to give up looking for him. Just then, she heard a rustling sound. The sound came from a few feet in front of her on the left hand side. Jordan assumed straight away that this was the stranger because surely it couldn't be anything else. Slowly Jordan walked towards the sound. When she got to the spot she tried looking through the hedge to see what or who had made the sound. Just then, Jordan felt a hand on her shoulder. She nearly jumped out of her skin and she spun round to see who it was.

"Bloody hell, Lucas, you scared me!" said Jordan.

"Sorry about that, but I thought you were following someone."

"I am, but he spotted me and he came down this road. Now, I'm sure he is hiding behind this bush."

Lucas decided to go behind the bush to see if there was anyone there while Jordan stayed where she was on the off chance that she saw the stranger.

"Jordan, are you there?" said Lucas.

"Yes, I am," said Jordan.

"Well, I can't see anyone. Are you sure he came behind here?"

"No, I'm not sure but he can't be anywhere else because he disappeared so quickly. Can you keep looking, just to be sure?"

So, Lucas carried on looking. Jordan could hear Lucas walking behind the hedge looking for the stranger. For the next couple of minutes all Jordan could hear was Lucas's footsteps behind the hedge. Then, Lucas shouted at someone. Then, this person set off running and Lucas set off running after them. Jordan could hear what was happening and she set off running in the same direction as their footsteps. The stranger found a gap in the hedge and he went through it, appearing just a few feet in front of Jordan. Now, the chase was really on. When Lucas came from behind the hedge he saw which direction Jordan and the stranger were running and he tried his best to keep up. As Lucas was trying to keep up he pulled out his mobile phone and called the station for backup.

While Lucas was calling for back up Jordan had chased the stranger into a smallish shopping centre. For a few seconds Jordan had lost sight of the stranger and couldn't see where he had gone. Most of the shops had already closed, but there were a few still open. By now, Lucas had caught up with Jordan. She told Lucas that she had lost sight of the stranger for a few seconds but he had to be somewhere close.

The first thing the two of them did was to check in the shops that were still open. There were seven shops that were still open and they took one each. When they had been in the first six shops there was no sign of the stranger, so they went into the seventh shop together. By now, the backup that Lucas had called for had arrived. As Jordan and Lucas went into the shop the officers stayed outside and looked for anyone acting strangely. As the two of them walked into the shop the shopkeeper walked up to them.

"You're lucky, I was about to lock up," said the shopkeeper.

"That's okay, we won't be long. I'm DS Lucas and this is Jordan Lewis, we were wondering if anyone has come in here within the last few minutes?" said Lucas.

"Yes, I rent the flat upstairs and the tenant has just come in and gone upstairs."

"Would it be possible to go upstairs and have a chat with him?" said Lucas.

"Of course you can, I will show you where to go."

The shopkeeper showed them the way to the flat. They couldn't find anyone on the landing, so they asked the shopkeeper to let them in. As they entered the flat they heard the toilet being flushed, then the bathroom door opened and the tenant came walking out.

"Who the hell are you and what are you doing in my flat?" said the tenant.

"I'm DS Lucas and this is Jordan Lewis, we are looking into the case of the pocket watch killer," said Lucas.

"What do you want with me, then?" said the tenant.

"I was wondering if you could tell us what you've been doing for the last twenty minutes or so?" said Lucas.

"Yeah, I've been working for the last twelve hours and it's taken me a little over twenty minutes to get home."

"Whereabouts do you work?" said Lucas.

"King Cone the traffic cone place."

"Yeah I know the place and what did you say your name was?" said Lucas.

"I didn't but it's Joe Crammer."

"Any relation to David Crammer who lives on the caravan park?" said Jordan.

"Yeah he's my brother, why do you ask?"

"Oh, no reason," said Jordan.

"Well, that's all for now, thanks for your time," said Lucas.

At that the two of them went downstairs, thanked the shopkeeper and left the shop. When they were outside they stopped and had a chat.

"So, what do you think, he seems believable to me?" said Lucas.

"Yeah, he does seem believable and he appears to be different to the one we've been chasing. The one we've been chasing looks a lot broader," said Jordan.

At that, Jordan and Lucas made their way back to their cars. Just before they did that, Lucas told the other officers to go back to their jobs. Unbeknown to them Joe was watching them from his flat window. As he watched them walk away Joe had a little smile to himself, then he moved away from the window.

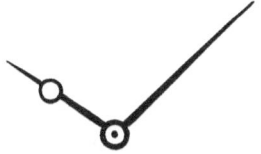

CHAPTER ELEVEN

N ow, it was the following morning. The killer had been awake for an hour. He'd had some of the food he had with him for his breakfast and now he was thinking about making a move out of the area. It was almost seven o'clock but it was still quite quiet so the killer decided to make a move before it started to get busy. First, he needed to make sure that no one was around. He slowly came out of his hiding place and had a good look around. Then he quickly grabbed his things and started to make his way out of the area.

"Where are you planning on going, you can't go too far," said the voice. The killer just ignored the voice. He was too close to the latest murder scene and the killer knew that he had to put as much distance between himself and the scene as possible.

The one thing that he was really curious about was whether the police were still watching his caravan. From where he was the caravan park was only about three miles away so it wouldn't take too long to walk there. Plus, with him knowing Cornwall so well he knew of a few shortcuts. "This isn't a good idea, the police could be waiting for you," said the voice. As the killer made his way to the caravan park his eyes were everywhere. The last thing he wanted was to be seen by the police.

Now, he was about half a mile away from the caravan park. So far, he'd only seen a couple of people on his journey and there had been no sign of the police. But just then he heard some sirens. He couldn't tell if they were the police or not or which direction they were coming from. All the time the sirens were getting closer and closer. By now the killer was quickly looking around for somewhere to hide just in case it was the police. Before he could find somewhere to hide he saw in the distance an ambulance travelling in his direction with its lights and sirens going. He breathed a sigh of relief. After he had watched the ambulance drive by, the killer walked the remaining half a mile to the caravan park.

At the entrance to the caravan park he stopped for a moment to check and make sure that the police weren't there any more. When he was completely satisfied and happy that they weren't there, the killer made his way quickly to his caravan, unlocked the door and rushed inside. From the inside, he looked to see if he could see anyone watching him, but there wasn't. "This is a real bad idea," said the voice. The killer couldn't care less that it was a bad idea because he needed a shower and to wash some of his clothes. The first thing he did was to put his dirty clothes in the washer. When he had done that he went through the kitchen cupboards and took out all the tin food he could find and put them in bags. He did this because he wasn't staying at the caravan and he didn't want to run out of food. When he had sorted the food he went to have a shower. "You are taking too long. What if the police come back," said the voice. The killer took no notice.

After his shower and when he was dressed, the killer turned on the radio so he could listen to the news. As he listened to the radio he made himself a cup of coffee. When he'd finished making his coffee the news came on the radio. The main story on the news was about the pocket watch killer. The killer listened intently. The news reader was telling the public about the latest victim. The killer was waiting to hear what would be said about the police investigation. While he was waiting he heard a noise from outside. The first thing he thought the noise could be was the police, so he went to have a look. He didn't get too close to the window because if it was the police he didn't want to be seen by them. When he looked through the window he couldn't see anything at first, but when he looked at the caravan opposite he saw David Crammer, his neighbour. David seemed to be behaving strangely as if he was nervous about something and the killer couldn't work out why.

David went in to his caravan but left the door open. Through the caravan windows the killer could see David doing something but he couldn't see what. After a few minutes David came back out with a shoulder bag over his right shoulder. He then closed and locked the caravan door and started to walk away. By the direction that David was walking, the killer knew that he was leaving the caravan park via the back exit.

By now, the killer's washer was just finishing so he took the wet clothes out and put them in the dryer. When he had done that he made himself another cup of coffee and went to sit down. As he was sat there, he heard something else outside. When he went to have a look through the window he could see Jordan looking at David's caravan. "That's the PI. Make sure that she doesn't see you and turn off the dryer because she might hear it," said the voice. The killer turned off the dryer, then he went back to watch Jordan. The killer could see that Jordan was really interested in David's caravan for some reason. Just in front of the killer's caravan was Jordan's car and she returned to sit in it. After a few minutes of sitting in her car, Jordan then started the engine and drove away. He breathed a sigh of relief. The killer gave it a few minutes, to make sure Jordan wasn't coming back, then, he turned the dryer back on. With Jordan coming back to the caravan park the killer knew he couldn't hang around too long in his caravan.

As soon as the dryer was finished he packed the clothes into bags, made sure he had enough food and everything else that he needed before making his way out of the caravan. Before he left, however, he looked through the window one last time to check Jordan hadn't returned. When he was happy that the coast was clear, he left the caravan, closed and locked the door and left the caravan park.

The killer wasn't sure where he was going to go but he did know Cornwall very well and he was sure he could find the perfect hiding place. Then, he had an idea. He thought that he would go back to the barn to see if the police were still there. He knew of a way of getting there which would give a good chance of not being seen. "It may be a good idea to go to the barn. If the police have left they may not return there," said the voice.

While the killer was making his way to the barn Joe Crammer was at his job at the traffic cone factory. As he was working he was thinking about the visit from the police the previous night. Joe was now beginning to wonder if his brother David had anything to do with the pocket watch murders. Just then he noticed David walking into the factory. For a moment David stood there and looked around. When he saw Joe at his machine he walked over to him.

"What are you doing here?" said Joe.

"I just thought that I would let you know that I'm leaving the area for a little while," said David.

"Yeah and why's that?"

"Because the police and this private investigator think that I have something to do with the pocket watch murders."

"Yeah, they came to see me last night."

"What did they want with you?"

"Someone was seen in the caravan opposite yours and they thought it may have been me. Don't you think it may look suspicious you leaving all of a sudden?"

"No, of course not, if anyone asks say that I've gone on holiday somewhere. Okay, I'd better get going. Here are the keys to my caravan – could you keep an eye on it for me?"

Joe said that he would but when he asked David where he was going David wouldn't tell him. This was because David didn't want the police to find out. By now, the killer had reached the barn. Before he went right up to the barn he found somewhere he couldn't be seen. When he had found the perfect spot he had a real good look around to see if he could see any sign of the police – and he couldn't. He waited a few minutes longer to be absolutely certain. When he was totally happy that the police weren't there, he made his way to the barn. The killer targeted the back of the barn where he knew the window would be unlocked. As soon as he was at the window he got it open as quickly as he could. He put the bags inside and then he got himself inside. When he was inside he closed the window and made himself comfortable.

When the killer had been in the barn for only a minute or so he could hear voices coming from outside. The more he listened the more he was sure the voices were coming from the back of the barn. He went to the back window to see if he could get a glimpse of who it was. When he got to the window and looked to his right he could see a couple of people whom he recognised straight away – it was the two ramblers that spoke to him a few days ago. "Quick, lock the window and get out of sight just in case they come to the window," said the voice. The killer did just that, he locked the window and went to hide behind some boxes that were near the front of the barn.

While he was behind the boxes he could still hear the voices of the ramblers. Then, he heard something at the back of the barn. The noise he could hear sounded like someone was trying to open the window. At this point, the killer decided to have a little look to see what was happening. When he peered round the boxes he could see the ramblers at the window. "They must have seen you climb through the window. They could go to the police. What are you going to do about it?" said the voice. He sat there thinking about what he should be doing for the best. "You can't take the chance that they didn't see you and won't report you. Do something," said the voice. When he looked round the boxes he could see that the two of them were still at the window but they were facing away. The killer took the chance to get closer to the window. When he was at the window he stood to one side of it so that he wouldn't be seen, but now he could hear them talking more clearly.

"This is a strange place to have a barn," said the man.

"I wonder who it belongs to?" said the woman.

"I don't have a clue. Come, on let's carry on with our walk," said the man.

At that, the two of them started to walk away. From what he heard them say he gathered that they hadn't seen him climb through the window and they had no idea that he was even there. "You've had some luck there," said the voice. The killer had to agree that he had a fair degree of luck to get away with that one.

After this he decided not to spend all his time in the barn because he knew that the police, Jordan the PI or even the ramblers could come back at any time. He knew of a couple of hiding places that were near the barn but were out of sight where he could pitch his tent. When he had given the ramblers enough time to get out of the area he went to one of those places.

About three hundred yards away from the barn there was the perfect place for him to pitch his tent. It was in a slight dip in the ground and it was surrounded by bushes. It also had a really good view of the barn, so he could see if anyone came to the barn.

While the killer was pitching his tent, Jordan had finished her breakfast and was having a drive around;

this time she had Jarvis with her. Jarvis suggested to Jordan that they go back to the caravan park to see if David Crammer had returned to his caravan yet. She had been there a little earlier in the day to see if he was there and he wasn't, but she couldn't see the harm in going again. On the journey to the caravan park the two of them kept looking around on the off chance that they saw David. Soon, they were at the caravan park. When Jordan had parked the car the two of them went over to David's caravan to see if he was home. Jordan knocked on the door but there was no answer. The two of them looked through the windows but the lights were off and they couldn't see any movement. Now, Jordan was becoming frustrated because she really wanted to talk to David. Jordan thought it might be an idea if they sat in the car and waited a while just in case David showed up. As they were walking back to the car, Joe Crammer, David's brother, came walking onto the caravan park. When Joe saw Jordan he knew that she was looking for David.

"Are you not working today, Joe?" said Jordan.

"I was working this morning. I've just booked half a day off because I'm not feeling too good," said Joe.

"What are you doing here, then?" said Jordan.

"David's caravan is on my way home and I thought that I would come and chill out here for a while with David before I went home."

"We've just had a look and David isn't home," said Jordan.

"That's okay, I have a key," said Joe.

"Do you have any idea where he is?"

"I don't have a clue."

"Would it be okay if we come in to have a look around and see if he left any clue of where he's gone?" said Jordan.

"Yeah, if you want," said Joe.

Joe only agreed because it would look suspicious if he said no. Joe unlocked the door, opened it and went walking in with Jordan and Jarvis following closely behind. The actual reason Jordan wanted to go into the caravan was to see if David was in there or not. Joe offered them something to drink but the two of them declined, saying that they were okay. After a few minutes of looking around Jordan could tell that David wasn't there and she couldn't see anything that would give her a clue as to where he might be. At this point, Jordan knew that it was a waste of time them being there, so she thanked Joe and both she and Jarvis left the caravan. Joe watched them go back to the car, and when Jordan started to drive away he breathed a sigh of relief.

As they were driving from the caravan park Jordan was thinking about Joe. She was certain that he knew more than he was letting on. Then, her mind drifted to the main suspect in the case; she began to wonder where he may be and what he was up to. Wherever he was Jordan knew he couldn't be too far away.

While Jordan and Jarvis were driving around on the lookout for their next lead, Lucas was just arriving at the station. He was already thinking about the day ahead and what may happen. He was hoping for something that would lead him in the right direction. He had barely got to his desk when the phone started to ring. When he answered it was Jane Brown, the CSI, calling him and she was really excited.

"What are you all excited about?" said Lucas.

"The fingerprint that I found at the latest victim's house has given me a name and a face," said Jane.

"Yeah, who is it?"

"It's someone called Mike O'Brien and he has a record for violence."

"Can you email me all the information?"

"Yeah, I will do it right now."

When the call finished, Lucas turned on his computer and the email from Jane had already come in. When he opened the email the first thing he saw was the photo of the person that the fingerprint belonged to. When he read the details that were with the photo he saw that the person's name was Mike O'Brien and he had a long list of criminal convictions, all of which were for violence. Then, when Lucas read further he saw that O'Brien was a diagnosed psychopath. He also read that O'Brien had spent his last sentence in a mental hospital. Lucas knew that he had to get O'Brien's face out to the public and the best way to do that was to make up wanted posters. Before he went down this route he would have to go to O'Brien address to see if he had an explanation for the fingerprint, but O'Brien's address wasn't known. So, he made a start on the wanted posters. First, though, he gave Jordan a call to let her know about the new lead.

As soon as Jordan heard about the new lead she made her way straight round to the station. She wasn't far from the station so it wouldn't take her too long to get there. Lucas didn't say too much about the new lead, which made Jordan really curious. Jordan very quickly parked her car and Jordan and Jarvis made their way in. The officer on the front desk called up to Lucas who said he was expecting them and then they were let up.

Jordan and Jarvis soon made their way upstairs. When they were in the right place they couldn't see Lucas anywhere. As they stood there looking around for Lucas he came walking into the room behind them.

"You got here quickly," said Lucas.

The two of them turned around and Jordan said, "Yes, we were eager to know what this new evidence is."

"It is fingerprint evidence," said Lucas.

"Yeah, do you have a name to go with the print?" said Jordan excitedly.

"Yes, a name and a face. Come over here and I will show you."

Lucas took them to a printing machine where an officer was printing off some wanted posters. Lucas took one of the posters and gave it to Jordan.

"This Mike O'Brien is now our prime suspect," said Lucas.

"I see he has a long list of convictions, all of which are for violence," said Jordan.

"Yes, he has. I also believe he is the same person who left the pocket watch in the reception area of the station," said Lucas.

"Really?" said Jordan.

"I wasn't up here when you arrived because I was at my car – I left the photo of the person in the reception area in the car," said Lucas.

Lucas put that photo alongside the photo on the wanted poster and the three of them compared the two. With the reception photo being a little fuzzy the three of them struggled

to tell if the two photos were of the same person. The person
in the reception photo had their head down which didn't
help matters. Jordan asked if she could keep a wanted poster
of O'Brien so that she could go looking for him and Lucas
agreed. At that, Jordan and Jarvis made their way out of
the station and to the car. On the way to the car Jordan
kept studying the photo of O'Brien. The more she looked
at O'Brien, the more she thought she recognised him from
somewhere. When they were back at the car, Jordan asked
Jarvis if he could drive for a while which he was pleased to do.

"Where do you want to go first?" said Jarvis.

"Head towards Penzance, I've a feeling we may find
something there."

"Ah, that Jordan Lewis feeling!"

Jordan smiled then went back to looking at O'Brien's
photo. For some reason she couldn't shake the feeling that
she had seen O'Brien somewhere before, but she couldn't
think where. Jordan looked up from the photo and started to
look around. She was hoping to get lucky and get a glimpse
of O'Brien. Just then, she saw Joe Crammer, David's brother,
walking down the road instead. Jordan asked Jarvis to pull
over because she wanted to show Joe the wanted poster of
O'Brien. Jarvis found a place to park a little further up the
road and pulled over. Once the car was stopped Jordan got
out and started to walk towards Joe.

"What do you want now?" said Joe.

"I was wondering if you know the person in this
photo?" said Jordan.

Joe looked at the wanted poster and said, "Yeah, he
lives on the caravan park. He actually lives in the caravan
opposite David's."

"Thank you, that's a real big help," said Jordan.

Jordan went back to the car, got in and asked Jarvis to take her back to the station. On the way back Jordan sent a text to Lucas telling him that she was on her way back to the station. It didn't take them long. When they were in the reception area they were allowed to go straight up to see Lucas. When they were upstairs Jordan could see Lucas talking to several uniformed officers. He was telling them to get out and about putting up the wanted posters. Within two or three minutes of them arriving back Lucas had finished telling the officers what he wanted them to do. When he had finished they went to put out the wanted posters. Then, Lucas noticed Jordan and Jarvis waiting to speak with him.

"So, your text said that you could have a possible lead," said Lucas.

"Yes, while we were driving away from here earlier we noticed Joe Crammer, David's brother. So, we pulled over to have a chat with him. When we showed him the wanted poster of O'Brien and asked if he knew O'Brien he said that he did. According to Joe, O'Brien lives on the caravan park right opposite David's caravan," said Jordan.

"That's interesting," said Lucas.

"It's certainly worth looking into," said Jordan.

Jordan told Lucas that she would go and check O'Brien's caravan on the off chance that he may have returned. Then, both she and Jarvis made their way down to the car. As they were doing that the killer, now known as Mike O'Brien, had pitched his tent; he then made himself as comfortable as possible. Where he had decided to pitch his tent was in a slight dip in the ground, surrounded by

THE POCKET WATCH KILLER

bushes and about a hundred feet or so away from the barn. "That was a close call with the ramblers, you will have to be careful," said the voice. O'Brien was blissfully unaware that the police and Jordan had found out who he was and they were actively looking for him.

The ramblers who had spoken to O'Brien were in a café having something to eat and noticed a police officer come in. The officer had a little chat with the owner, then, the officer started to leave. Just before he left he put something in the window. The ramblers could see that it was some kind of poster but they couldn't see what was on it because it was facing the street. When they finished their meal they left the café. Before they went anywhere they had a look at the poster that the officer had put up and straight away they recognised the photo of O'Brien. On the poster they also noticed a phone number to call and Lucas's name for them to ask for. One of them got their mobile phone out of their pocket, called the number on the poster and asked for Lucas. When they were put through to Lucas they told them everything they knew. Instantly, Lucas asked them to come to the station to give a statement. So, they made their way to the station as quickly as they could.

While the ramblers were making their way to the station, Jordan and Jarvis were having a drive around with Jordan driving. While they were travelling the two of them were looking around for O'Brien. Jordan was driving to the caravan park on the off chance that O'Brien had returned home, but then she had a change of heart. She had been at O'Brien's caravan a little earlier and he wasn't there. Then, she remembered about the barn and that she hadn't checked there for a while. So, she made her way to the barn instead.

Soon, they had arrived at the path that led to the barn. When Jordan had parked the car the two of them got out and started to walk down the path towards the barn. Within a few minutes the two of them could see the barn. What they didn't know was O'Brien was already there. Jordan already knew that the barn doors were locked but the window at the back of the barn was unlocked. So, they made their way round to the window.

As they were walking to the back of the barn the two of them were talking and O'Brien could hear their voices. When he heard the voices he had a look to see who it was. When he saw that it was Jordan he made sure he got himself out of sight. "That's the PI, what's she doing here. You need to do something," said the voice. O'Brien got himself into a position where he could watch Jordan and Jarvis but so that they couldn't see him. O'Brien could see Jordan climbing through the window. When Jordan was in the barn and Jarvis was watching what she was doing, O'Brien took the chance to get a little closer. Within a few seconds O'Brien was at the corner of the barn. He stood at the side of the barn so Jarvis couldn't see him but he was able to peer round so he could see what was happening. Just then, O'Brien stood on a twig and it snapped. When Jarvis heard this he turned to see what it was. Jarvis felt a little nervous because this was the killer's barn, so he called out to Jordan.

"Jordan, I think someone is out here," said Jarvis.

Jordan then made her way out of the barn to check it out and have a look around. For a moment O'Brien stood there with his back pressed against the barn. "Quick, she's coming. Do something!" said the voice. O'Brien knew he had to get out of sight. He wanted to go to his tent which was out of sight but he knew that he couldn't go straight to it because he would be seen by Jordan and Jarvis. So, he ran directly in front towards the trees. When he was far enough into the trees O'Brien made his way round to his tent. "I hope they didn't see you," said the voice.

As O'Brien was making his way back to his tent Jordan and Jarvis were having a look around. O'Brien was lucky neither of them saw him run to the trees and out of sight. But Jarvis was adamant that he had heard someone, which was enough for Jordan to have a good look around. But they couldn't see anyone. Then, the two of them had a look around within the trees but again they couldn't see anyone. So they decided to go a little further away from the barn. What they didn't realise was that they were walking towards O'Brien and his tent, but he was so well hidden they couldn't see him. For a moment or so the two of them stood there and looked around.

"I think whoever you heard is out of the area by now," said Jordan.

"Yeah, they must be," said Jarvis.

At that, the two of them turned and started to walk away. All the while O'Brien was watching them. "You're riding your luck, you need to be more careful," said the voice.

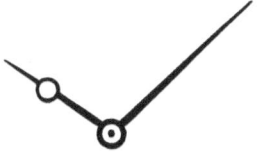

CHAPTER TWELVE

M ark Barker, the local journalist, was at his desk at home and was thinking about the pocket watch killer. At this point he didn't know that the police had found out the killer's name. Mark was wondering where he could go or what he could do to get more information about the case. He wasn't in the mood to just sit there and do nothing so he went for a drive.

Mark had been driving around for about forty-five minutes but not much was happening. While he was driving around he did notice what appeared to be some posters on lamp posts and in shop windows. So, the next one he came across on a lamp post he stopped to have a look at it. He could see it was a police wanted poster for the pocket watch killer. When he saw the photo and the name of Mike O'Brien he realised two things. Firstly, that the police had found out who the killer was and secondly, he seemed to recognise O'Brien from somewhere. He took a photo of the wanted poster on his phone so he could remind himself of the information at any time.

When he was happy with the photo, Mark returned to his car. For the next few minutes he sat there thinking. He was thinking whether O'Brien knew that the police now knew who he was. Then, he started to wonder where O'Brien might be. So, Mark started to drive around again. He then realised that O'Brien may be hiding out somewhere that the police have already searched like the barn for instance so he made his way to the barn in the hope that he would discover some information for his story. Little did he know that he was going to discover more than he could imagine.

On the journey to the barn Mark was looking everywhere on the off chance that he caught a glimpse of O'Brien. Soon, he was at the barn. When he was out of his car he paused for a moment. As he was stood there he started to think what he would do if O'Brien was actually here. Little did he know but O'Brien was already at the barn. Mark wondered what he should do for the best, go to the barn to have a look or get back in his car and leave.

"To hell with it, I will never get a good story by being timid," Mark thought to himself.

At that, Mark started to walk down the path towards the barn. He knew that O'Brien could be at the barn or somewhere within the area so he was looking everywhere. The last thing he wanted was to be surprised by O'Brien. Before he knew it, Mark was at the other end of the path and he could see the barn.

O'Brien at this point was in his tent trying to relax. He had no idea that Mark was at the barn. As Mark was walking round the barn he accidentally kicked a stone which hit the barn. "What was that noise, go and have a look," said the voice. O'Brien very quietly got out of his tent to have a look to see what had made the noise. At first, he couldn't see anything, but then he spotted Mark.

"He's that reporter that is doing a story about you, you can't let him find you," said the voice. O'Brien could see that Mark was just looking around the area of the barn. From where he was, O'Brien wasn't sure what Mark was looking for, but he was pleased that Mark wasn't looking in his direction.

Mark made his way to the window at the back of the barn. When he reached it he stood there and looked in for a few minutes. He was looking in to see if O'Brien was inside moving around. Little did Mark know but O'Brien was just a hundred feet away watching him. While Mark was looking through the window, O'Brien took the opportunity to move a little closer. Just a few feet from where Mark was stood was a quite a large bush and O'Brien managed to hide behind it without being seen. When Mark had been stood at the window for a few minutes he didn't see any movement and he was deciding if he would go inside for a look around. After a moment's thought he decided to have a look around inside because he was really curious to know exactly what was inside the barn.

As Mark tried opening the window he saw that it was unlocked and he slid it across. As he was about to climb through the window Mark heard something – it sounded like someone sneezing. With Mark knowing that the barn belonged to the killer Mark became really nervous because he knew the sneeze could have come from O'Brien. On hearing the sneeze Mark didn't want to take the chance of being cornered inside the barn by O'Brien, so he decided to leave the barn and move away from the area.

As he was walking back round to the front of the barn, Mark was looking everywhere on the off chance he caught a glimpse of O'Brien. Mark passed within a couple of feet of the bush that O'Brien was hiding behind but he failed to see him. When he was at the front of the barn Mark started to walk back up the path towards his car. As Mark made his way up the path O'Brien came from behind the bush and started to follow Mark. When Mark was only a short way up the path he could hear footsteps behind him. Assuming it was O'Brien that was behind him, he quickened his pace so that he could get to his car. Soon, they were at the other end of the path but as Mark went to his car O'Brien stayed within the treeline so that he wouldn't be seen. As O'Brien watched Mark drive away the voice spoke to him. "He knows it was you and now he's going to get the police. You can't stay here now, what are you going to do about it?" said the voice.

As Mark drove away O'Brien went back to his tent. When he was there he started to pack his things together. All the time he was wondering where would be the best place for him to go. Soon, he had everything packed away, including his tent. For the time being O'Brien didn't really want to go too far away from where he already was. About another two hundred feet from where he was the treeline became thicker and there were plenty of hiding places for him. So, he gathered his things together and he made his way to the trees. Within moments he had found the ideal spot among the trees and he started to make himself comfortable. Where he was he was very well hidden and he still had a good view of the barn. Before he put his tent up again he wanted to make sure Mark didn't return with the police, so he waited for a while to see what, if anything, would happen.

While O'Brien was making himself comfortable Mark was still in his car driving away from the area. Mark needed to tell someone about what had just happened but he was unsure who to tell, either Jordan or the police. When he had first met Jordan he had a good feeling about her so he decided to go and see her instead of the police. Mark remembered that Jordan had given him her business card so when he had found himself a parking spot he pulled over and gave her a call.

"Hi Jordan, this is Mark Barker the journalist that you've spoken to."

"Oh yes, I remember. How can I help?"

"Well, I think that I've stumbled onto the location of Mike O'Brien, the pocket watch killer."

"Yeah, where?"

"The old barn, the one that is believed to be owned by him. Do you want me to come and get you?"

"No, I know where that is, I will meet you there," she said.

At that, the two of them hung up. Jordan was in her room at the bed and breakfast. She very quickly put her jacket on, grabbed her car keys and mobile phone and then she made her way down to her car. Jarvis was out somewhere with Carl and she didn't want to disturb them so she went to meet Mark alone. Within a few minutes of Mark's call Jordan was in her car heading to the barn. All the way to the barn Jordan was wondering if O'Brien would still be there. If he was this would be an opportunity for Jordan to close the case and have a serial killer put behind bars.

Soon, Jordan was arriving at the path that led to the barn. As she was pulling up she saw Mark leaning against his car. She walked over to Mark and they chatted, then the two of them headed down the path towards the barn. Knowing that O'Brien could be in the area Jordan's eyes were everywhere. Just then, a bird flew right in front of her. This scared her so much she almost screamed. Once she had calmed down, they carried on walking towards the barn.

When the barn came into sight the two of them slowly walked out into the open. They looked around to see if there was any sign of O'Brien, but there wasn't, so they made their way round to the back. As soon as they were round the back of the barn the two of them felt a sudden change in the atmosphere, a change as if something was going to happen. They got the feeling that O'Brien wasn't too far away.

And indeed, O'Brien was still around – he was still hiding within the trees and he had noticed them come to the back of the barn. "See, I told you he would call someone. What are you going to do now?" said the voice. O'Brien stood there and watched the two of them intently because he really wanted to know what they were up to.

Jordan started to look around for any possible evidence of O'Brien recently being in the area. She was looking on the ground for the remains of any recent camp fires because she had a gut feeling that O'Brien would be camping. She felt this because it would make it easy for him to move around and evade the police – she just didn't know how right she was.

Slowly the two of them were moving towards where O'Brien had pitched his tent, all the while being watched by him. When they were in the right spot they saw the remains of a recent camp fire. Jordan now knew that she was on to something. She had a look in and around the camp fire to see if there was any evidence of O'Brien being there, but there wasn't anything specific. When Jordan was happy that there was nothing else to see the two of them moved on, this time walking towards the trees where O'Brien was hiding. Step by step the two of them were getting closer to him. "They're getting closer, what are you going to do about it?" said the voice. O'Brien knew he had to do something. He didn't want to challenge them because with there being two of them they could overpower him and he would be caught. So, he started to look around for the best way for him to escape.

By now, Jordan and Mark were entering the trees where O'Brien was hiding. "Quick, you got to do something," said the voice. O'Brien saw a good way to escape, so he grabbed his things and tried to make his way out of the area. Just then, Jordan saw some movement. On the off chance that it may have been O'Brien, Jordan went to have a look. Little did she know that it was actually O'Brien that she had seen walking away. O'Brien glanced over his shoulder and saw Jordan coming in his direction, so he picked up his pace to get away from her. The problem he had was that Jordan had already seen him and she had a very good idea that this was O'Brien that she was following. By now Mark had also seen what was happening and he started to follow the two of them.

The direction they were going in was towards a railway track, about three quarters of a mile away and O'Brien knew that there would be plenty of hiding places on the other side of the track. So, he tried to reach there as soon as he could. Jordan was trying her best to catch up with him but O'Brien would duck out of sight. This was making it quite difficult for her to follow him.

As they were beginning to approach the track, O'Brien was beginning to tire, but he was determined to make it. When they were very near the track a train could be heard. It was a very long freight train. O'Brien was lucky – he managed to cross the tracks to the other side before the train reached them – but Jordan and Mark weren't so lucky.

"Damn it, I'm sure that was O'Brien," said Jordan.

"Yeah, it was. The killer has just gotten lucky," agreed Mark.

Frustration was all over them as they stood there watching the train go by. It was such a long train and it was only travelling at a slow speed so it took a few minutes to pass them. All the while O'Brien was getting further and further away. Eventually the train had passed and the two of them were able to cross the track. When they were on the other side of the track there was a bank that went about twenty feet down; in front of them they could see nothing but trees and they had no idea where O'Brien was.

"He could be anywhere," said Mark.

"Yeah, we'll never find him in there," said Jordan.

After standing there for a moment or so the two of them turned around and started to walk away. Little did they know that they were being watched, but it wasn't the killer – there was a stranger lurking and he was circling with intent. When the two of them had walked far enough away the stranger came out of hiding and started to follow them.

Jordan and Mark went back the same way they had come and they talked about how close they had been to catching O'Brien. Then, it dawned on Jordan that it might be a good idea to tell Lucas about what had just happened as he could bring several officers with him to search the trees.

Lucas arranged for a team of officers and they would meet her and Mark at the barn. When she had finished the call she and Mark continued their way to the barn, totally unaware that they were being followed.

Before too long the two of them were back at the barn and they waited for Lucas to arrive. The stranger had followed them to the barn but remained out of sight. Jordan noticed five tree stumps that were close together and she and Mark decided to sit on a couple while they waited for Lucas. While they sat there they started to talk about the case. What they didn't know was just a few feet from where they were sat the stranger that had followed them from the train tracks was hiding behind a large tree not too far from them. While Jordan and Mark were talking Jordan received a call on her mobile. When she answered it, it was Jarvis asking where she was. She went on to tell him what was happening. In the meantime, Mark went for a walk around the area of the barn. From where he was standing the stranger could hear everything that Jordan was saying.

Jordan, while still talking to Jarvis, stood up to walk over to Mark to see what he was up to. As she did so she heard something behind her. At first, she didn't think anything of it, but then, she heard it again. Out of curiosity she went to investigate. The stranger saw her coming and he tried to keep out of sight. Now, Jordan was a matter of inches away from the stranger and was about to see him when she heard her name being called. When she turned around to see who it was she saw that it was Lucas. She told Jarvis that Lucas had arrived and she would call him back later. When she had put her phone away and started to walk towards Lucas, the stranger gave a sigh of relief.

Jordan noticed that Lucas had brought quite a few officers with him. She once again told him exactly what had happened with Mark confirming everything. When they had finished talking Jordan and Mark took Lucas and his officers to the railway tracks. The stranger saw what was happening so he got out of the way so that he wouldn't be seen. When he had found a suitable hiding place the stranger remained out of sight, but he was still able to watch them walk away from him. And then when they were far enough away the stranger came out of hiding and got himself out of the area.

Before too long, Jordan and everyone else reached the railway tracks. After a moment, to check that there wasn't a train coming, they all crossed the tracks. Then, Lucas asked all the officers to spread out and to walk through the trees to look for O'Brien, or any evidence of which way he had gone. Mark stayed with them as they searched for O'Brien because this would be really good for his story.

O'Brien was a good way into the trees and had found himself an excellent hiding place. Little did he know that Jordan had returned with the police and they were actively searching the area for him!

Jordan and the police were getting deeper and deeper into the trees. They weren't moving too quickly because they didn't want to miss anything. While Jordan and the police were moving slowly through the trees O'Brien was in his hiding spot. He had found what appeared to be a disused tree house. It was a real fluke that he had even noticed it – he just looked up at the right moment and saw it. The ladder was attached flush to the tree and wasn't really noticeable if you didn't know that it was there. The tree house inside was quite spacious and O'Brien was able to spread out. He hadn't had a good sleep for three or four days now, so he unrolled his sleeping bag, put his pillow at one end and tried to get some sleep.

For a while he struggled to get to sleep and he began to toss and turn. Eventually he drifted off to sleep. Within seconds of him falling asleep he began to dream. His dream began with him walking down a street. Then, from what appeared from nowhere, his first victim was stood in front of him. So, he turned and started to walk the other way. When he had walked only a few feet his second victim was stood in front of him, so he crossed the road. When he had reached the other side his third victim was stood there. Then, has he looked around, he was surrounded by all his victims. All of them were getting closer and closer to him. When they were close to him and they were about to grab him, O'Brien woke up. After a few seconds of confusion, he realised he had been dreaming.

As he was lying there thinking about his dream he heard something outside. For a moment he lay still, listening to the noise. Then, it dawned on him. The noise that he heard were voices and they were coming closer and closer. Curiosity got the better of him and he went to have a look. When he went through the door he was on the platform that the tree house was built on. At this point, O'Brien was on his hands and knees because he didn't want to be seen by whoever it was. The first thing that he saw was a line of police, then he saw Jordan and they were walking towards him. "I knew she would be back with the police. You'll have to be quiet and hope they don't notice the tree house," said the voice. O'Brien lay down to reduce the risk of him being seen and he watched Jordan and the police search for him. When they were practically under the tree house Lucas told everyone to stop and went over to Jordan to have a chat.

"O'Brien could be anywhere and we don't have the manpower to search the whole area before it goes dark," said Lucas.

"Yeah, you're right. He could be long gone by now," said Jordan.

At that, Jordan, Lucas and the other officers turned around and made their way back to their cars. None of them realised how close they were to O'Brien. "You were really lucky this time," said the voice.

Meanwhile, that stranger who had been lurking around was wandering about near the bed and breakfast where Jordan was staying. He was beginning to feel a little hungry so he went to a nearby chippy to get himself something to eat. While he was in the chippy the stranger could see the bed and breakfast. As he was waiting for his food he saw Jordan returning to the bed and breakfast.

When he had got his food the stranger left the chippy. Opposite the bed and breakfast there was a bench where the stranger could sit down and eat his food. As he passed the bed and breakfast he saw Jordan stood near the front door talking to someone on her mobile phone. The stranger sat on the bench, began to eat his food and started to watch Jordan.

When Jordan had finished her phone call she went into the bed and breakfast and up to her room. But she couldn't settle. Jordan was so unsettled she was unable to sit down so she began to pace the room. One time when she passed the window she stopped and looked out. As she was looking around at what was happening outside she noticed the stranger sat on the bench and how he kept looking at the bed and breakfast and specifically at her window. Curiosity got the better of her so she went down to have a chat with him.

Jordan put on her jacket, grabbed her room key and made her way downstairs. When she was in the reception area she saw Lucas. When he noticed her he approached her but before he had a chance to say anything Jordan asked him to wait a minute because she wanted to check something. However, outside she noticed the stranger had gone from the bench, and she couldn't see him anywhere. Disappointed that she was unable to talk to the stranger, she went back inside to talk to Lucas instead.

CHAPTER THIRTEEN

———

N ow, it was eight o'clock in the evening. Jordan was in her room at the bed and breakfast. She was sat in the armchair thinking about the case. This was one of the toughest cases of her career and she was beginning to wonder if she would ever solve it.

For a little while Jordan stopped thinking about the pocket watch killer and started to think about the stranger that seemed to be watching her. Something was telling her that the stranger had something to do with the case but she couldn't put her finger on it.

Jordan was beginning to feel a little restless and she couldn't bear being inside, so she decided on a walk to get some fresh air. She grabbed her jacket, mobile phone, her room key and made her way outside. She wanted to be alone for a while so she didn't bother telling Jarvis that she was going out. Jordan decided to go to the nearby beach, where one of the earlier murders had taken place. With it being summer and the sun still being in the sky there were still quite a few people out and about.

As she was walking to the beach Jordan was looking at everyone that was out. Jordan knew that O'Brien and the stranger could be nearby and she didn't want to miss them.

With no sign of O'Brien or the stranger, Jordan started to walk along the beach. Before long Jordan was deep in thought and became oblivious to the few people remaining on the beach. She was thinking about the stranger and what connection he had, if any, to the case.

As she was walking along the beach Jordan was totally unaware that someone had spotted her from the road. As Jordan was walking along she came across a large rocky area. She sat on one of the rocks and looked out to sea while thinking about the case. While she was sat there thinking, the person that had spotted her walked over to her.

"I thought it was you," he said.

"Lucas, what are you doing here?"

"I have finished work for the day and I'm not ready to go home just yet. This is my favourite beach and I decided to spend a little time here. It looked like you were deep in thought when I walked across to you."

Lucas sat on the rock next to Jordan and they started to talk about the case. As the two of them talked the stranger was nearby enjoying the nice weather. He had bought himself some fish and chips and was making his way to the beach where Jordan and Lucas were so that he could eat them. Even though he had some fish and chips earlier the fresh air made him hungry for some more. Before he actually got to the beach there were some benches and he sat on one of them. As he sat there eating his fish and chips the stranger looked over to the rocks. As he did so he noticed Jordan and Lucas. Knowing who the two of them were, he was curious to know what they were talking about. As the stranger ate his food he kept an eye on them because he didn't want them to walk off without him knowing.

When he had finished his fish and chips, he put his rubbish in a nearby bin, then he tried to get close enough to Jordan and Lucas to hear what they were talking about. Jordan and Lucas were still sat on the rock talking and weren't paying much attention to the people around them. This made it easy for the stranger to get by them unnoticed. When he was a few feet pastthem he went over the low wall and onto the rocks. As quickly as he could he got a little closer to them so that he could listen better to what they were talking about.

There was quite a large rock just behind Jordan and Lucas and that was where the stranger settled so he could listen to the two of them. He could tell that they were talking about the pocket watch killer. Just then, Jordan had a shiver go up and down her spine. It wasn't a particularly cold day and Jordan only usually shivered like that if something was going to happen or she was being watched.

"Are you okay?" said Lucas.

"I don't know. It felt like someone had just walked over my grave."

Lucas laughed at that then he saw that she was being serious.

"You're being serious, aren't you?"

"I don't know how this happens or why, but every time I'm working a case and I feel like this, something always happens."

"You never know, it could mean that there's going to be a break in the case this time," Lucas said with a smile.

"It could mean that, it could mean anything," said Jordan.

Just as Jordan finished talking the two of them heard a sneeze. The sneeze came from behind them and to their left slightly. Just then, a young boy jumped down from the rocks. When they saw him Jordan and Lucas assumed that it was the boy that had sneezed. The two of them decided to move away from the rocks and they started to walk along the beach. The stranger gave a sigh of relief because it was actually him that had sneezed.

At this point, the stranger had heard enough and he didn't want to run the risk of being seen, so he made his way home. At the same time, Jordan and Lucas were talking about the case. Mark Barker, the journalist, had been working late in the office and he was making his way home. Mark didn't feel ready to go home just yet, so he went for a drive around. He didn't drive anywhere in particular, he just drove around in the hope that he saw something that was connected with the pocket watch killer case that he was writing about.

At first, Mark started by driving around the general area. He had the car radio on and he was listening to the local station. The radio host was inviting local residents to call in and talk about the pocket watch killer that was tormenting Cornwall. There were a lot of angry people calling in. Most of the anger was aimed at the police for not catching the killer. Then, the station received a very strange call.

"Hello caller, tell everyone your views on the pocket watch killer," said the host.

A few seconds of silence followed, then, the caller started to talk in a shaky voice.

"I know who the killer is. The police will never catch him. This private investigator is on the right track but she is way behind," said the caller.

Then, the phone line went dead. As the host carried on with the show another member of staff at the station called the police and told them about the caller. At this point Lucas was informed and he made his way back to the station. All the while, Mark was sure that he recognised the voice of the caller.

Just then, Mark saw someone come out of a public phone box and rush away. Combined with what he had just heard on the radio, Mark thought this person was acting a little suspiciously. Luckily for Mark, this person was going in the same direction that he was. So, the first chance he got, Mark would park his car. Just a little way down the road there was a space for him to park so he pulled over and turned off the engine. Then, he looked in the wing mirror and saw the person from the phone box walking towards him.

When the person had passed, Mark got out of the car and started to follow them. As the two of them were walking along, the individual that Mark was following was looking around nervously. At one point, a police car came racing past with its lights and sirens blaring and this person nearly jumped out of their skin. Mark couldn't help but wonder why this person was so nervous. The only reason that Mark could really think of was that this person was involved in the case somehow, or at the very least knew something about it.

About twenty feet in front of them was a children's playground with swings, a slide and a roundabout. When they reached the playground the individual that Mark was following went into the playground and sat on one of the swings. For a moment Mark stood there and wondered what to do. Just past the entrance to the playground there was a bench, so Mark went and sat on it. As he sat down, the playground was behind him so he swivelled slightly on the bench. Now, he could see the playground and was able to watch the individual without making it obvious. As Mark was watching him he was swinging back and forwards gently and looking around as if he was waiting for someone.

Twenty minutes had gone by and he was still sat on the swing. But just then, someone came walking into the playground. As they walked past Mark was sure that he knew them from somewhere. When this individual was in the playground they went to the swings and sat next to the person that was already there. They were soon deep in conversation with one another. All the while Mark was trying to remember where he knew the other person from.

Then, it dawned on him: in the inside pocket of his coat there was a copy of the wanted poster. As he looked at the photo on the poster and then looked back at the person who had just arrived he was certain that it was the same person. He was certain that it was O'Brien who had just arrived. So, Mark took out his mobile phone from his jacket pocket and called the police.

As he was doing that Jordan and Lucas were arriving at the radio station. Jordan tagged along with Lucas because she was interested to hear about the phone call. When they were in the station they were shown into one of the offices. They were in the office for less than a minute when someone came in with some kind of recording device.

"I take it that you are the police," said the woman.

"Yes, I'm DS Mike Lucas, and this is Jordan Lewis, a private investigator who is looking into the case," said Lucas.

"I'm Jane Turnbull and I'm one of the producers here at the station. During our show this evening we had people calling in telling us their thoughts about the pocket watch killer. Well, during the show we received a very disturbing call," said Jane.

At that, Jane played the recording of the call for Jordan and Lucas to listen to. All the way through the short recording Lucas was certain that he knew the voice from somewhere. Something was telling him that it was someone that he had arrested before, but he couldn't remember what for.

As he was thinking about the person and who it could be, Lucas received a call from the police station. The station informed Lucas about the phone call from Mark Barker, the reporter, concerning the possible sighting of O'Brien and his location. When he had put his mobile away Lucas told Jordan about the sighting and the two made their way to the location. Just before they left, Jane Turnbull gave Lucas a recording of the phone call. As she did so he thanked her for her co-operation. At that, both he and Jordan made their way to the location of the sighting.

Jordan and Lucas couldn't get to the car quickly enough. They were really eager to see if the person that Mark had spotted was really O'Brien. Lucas knew exactly where Mark had spotted the individual and made his way there as quickly as he could. With him being a police officer and working in Cornwall for as long as he had, he had learned practically all the shortcuts in the area. Soon, they were arriving at the right place and they saw Mark watching someone. When Mark saw them pulling up he went over to them. He walked over to the passenger side of the car where Jordan was and she wound down the window.

"You may have bumped into O'Brien, then?" said Jordan.

"Yeah, I think he is one of the two guys that are sat on the swings in the playground behind me," said Mark.

"I've called the station for a couple of officers to back us up while we made our way here. We'll wait until they arrive before we go and talk to him, just in case it is O'Brien," said Lucas.

It would only be about five minutes before the officers that Lucas had asked for would arrive but it would be a nervous five minutes. The three of them didn't know how long the person who is thought to be O'Brien would stick around.

Before long a police car could be seen coming down the road. When the car reached where Lucas was standing and was pulling over, the person who was thought to be O'Brien started to leave the playground with his friend. As soon as Lucas saw this he went straight over to stop them.

"Excuse me, gentlemen, could you spare me a moment please?" said Lucas.

"What seems to be the problem?" said one.

"I'm DS Lucas and I'm working on the pocket watch killer case. We are talking to as many people as possible in an attempt to find the killer. I was wondering if I could see some ID."

As the two men were looking for their ID, Lucas was examining the two men and the one who looked like O'Brien in particular. When the two men handed over their IDs, Lucas had a real good look at them. But straight away he could see that neither of them were O'Brien and he had no reason to detain them, so he handed back their IDs.

"Okay, you can both go and thanks for your co-operation," said Lucas.

As the two men walked away they smiled to one another. Jordan had the funny feeling that she hadn't seen the last of the two men but chose to say nothing to Lucas. Just then, Jordan received a call on her mobile from Jarvis. Jarvis was concerned about her and wondered where she was, so Jordan said that she would tell him all about it once she was back at the bed and breakfast. At that, Lucas took Jordan back to the bed and breakfast and Mark made his own way home.

Meanwhile, O'Brien was heading back to the tree house. By now it was beginning to get dark and he wanted to reach the tree house before it was completely dark. For the last few hours the voice in his head had been quiet and he in himself was quite relaxed.

When he was about twenty-five to thirty feet from the tree house he saw some movement. At first, he couldn't really see who or what it was. Six to seven feet in front of him was a large tree, so he went to it so he wouldn't be seen just in case. Every so often he would peer round the tree to try and see who or what was moving around. One time when he peered round the tree he saw a person. This person seemed to be hovering near the tree with the tree house for some reason. Then, O'Brien saw another person who had a dog with them. At this point, the two people and the dog started to walk away from the tree with the tree house and they were actually walking towards O'Brien. As they walked past him O'Brien moved round the tree he was stood next to so that he wouldn't be seen.

When they had past O'Brien and were a good way in the distance O'Brien made his way back to the tree house. Unbeknown to O'Brien one of the people, for some reason, turned around and saw him then told the other person. The two of them had heard about the pocket watch killer and wondered if the person they were looking at was actually the killer. So the two of them with their dog hurried out of the area and made their way to the police station.

When he was at the right tree O'Brien made his way up to the tree house. When he was in the tree house he sat down and started to relax. But the voice started to talk to him. "You are going to have to keep watch tonight. Those people with the dog may have seen you, they may go and tell someone," said the voice. O'Brien ignored the voice and had a look at his food stash to see what he could have to eat.

While O'Brien was deciding what to eat the stranger that was keeping an eye on Jordan was at home watching TV. While he was watching the evening news came on. At the beginning of the news there was a story about the pocket watch killer. There was some footage of Jordan, Lucas and the police chasing O'Brien across the railway tracks and into the woods. Straight away the stranger knew the area that was being shown. Even though it was getting dark outside he was curious about it and he went to have a look. So, he grabbed his coat and a torch and went to see what he could find.

As the stranger was doing that Jarvis was sat in his room at the bed and breakfast and he too was watching the news. He was particularly interested in the footage of the pocket watch killer. When he had watched enough he went to have a chat with Jordan. But as he opened the door to his room he saw Jordan walking down the hall.

"Where have you been?" said Jarvis.

"I've just been out for a while thinking about the case," said Jordan.

At that the two of them went into Jarvis's room. The news was still reporting on the pocket watch killer. A video of one of the crime scenes was being aired. The crime scene was the one where the victim was found in her own home. The one thing that struck Jordan about the video was that to her it appeared to be the kind of video that was recorded on a mobile phone and not a professional camera crew. As they were watching they saw Mandy Fletcher the pathologist arrive and go into the house. Then, in the small crowd that had gathered Jordan saw someone that she felt shouldn't have been there. Jordan got a little closer to the TV to have a better look. When she did so she knew for certain that it was Carl Benson, Jarvis's friend who got them involved in the case.

"I wonder what Carl was doing there?" said Jordan.

"I have no idea. Didn't you see him whilst you were there?" said Jarvis.

"No I didn't and he didn't come over to me, neither."

"I will have to have a chat with him tomorrow and find out what is going on."

For the next hour or so Jordan stayed with Jarvis so the two of them could talk about the case. While they were doing that the stranger was making his way to the place that he had seen on the news. It was a fair way away from where he lived so he drove. By now it was becoming quite dark. But it was a pleasant evening without a cloud in the sky and the moon was big and bright. Where the stranger was heading the moonlight would be a real big help. As he drove he wondered if he would run into the killer. Now, he was beginning to have second thoughts because he was potentially going into a very dangerous situation. Several times he thought about turning around but for some strange reason he kept on driving. For some morbid reason he wanted to go and see what he could find.

Before long he had reached where he wanted to be. He had gone as far as he could by car, now he would have to walk the rest of the way. When he had parked his car and turned off the engine he sat there for a few minutes. The stranger wondered if what he was doing was the right thing. He knew how potentially dangerous it was but he was also intensely interested in finding where the killer was hiding out.

"Well, it's now or never," he said to himself.

At that, he grabbed his torch from the passenger seat and got out of the car. When he was happy that the car was locked he made his way to the railway tracks. With the moon being full and bright that really helped to light the way and he didn't need the torch just yet.

As he was making his way to the area he had seen on the news he remained highly vigilant, because he obviously didn't know where O'Brien was. At the moment it was really quiet and the stranger couldn't see or hear anything.

Before long the stranger was arriving at the railway tracks. From what he could see it was the same area of track that he saw on the news. After he looked both ways, to make sure that a train wasn't coming, the stranger crossed the tracks. When he had crossed the tracks he was faced with a wall of trees. Before he entered the trees he took a moment to gather his thoughts. He was really starting to think that this was a very stupid idea.

"Well, while I'm here I may as well continue," he said to himself.

At that, he made his way into the trees. Even though the moon was still full and bright the trees were blocking a lot of the light so the stranger had to use his torch. Knowing that O'Brien could be anywhere, the stranger was walking through the trees at a much slower pace. Just then, he heard something somewhere to his left. It was a snapping sound like someone had stood on a twig. Now, he was thinking that someone, possibly O'Brien, was nearby. The stranger was now becoming really unnerved.

"To hell with this, I'm getting out of here," said the stranger.

At that, he turned around and started to make his way back to the car. All the while he was looking around to make sure he wasn't being followed. Then, he heard another snapping sound. This made him think that he was being followed. By now, he couldn't get back to his car quickly enough. It wasn't long before he was back at the railway tracks but there was a train going by. It was a freight train which was very long and was going by very slowly. All the while he was waiting for the train to pass he was looking behind him to see if anyone was following him. Every passing moment he was waiting for the train to pass seemed to take an age, but eventually the train was through and the stranger could then cross the tracks. When he was back at his car he made his way out of the area as quickly as he could.

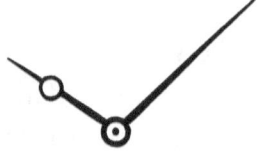

CHAPTER FOURTEEN

I t was now the following morning. The stranger was at home and was making himself some breakfast. As he was waiting for the kettle to boil he was thinking about the previous evening. He was wondering if the snapping sound that he had heard was a person or if it was actually an animal. He was still really curious to see what he could find out there and was thinking about going back there during the daytime.

Just then, the kettle finished boiling. He already had a cup ready with a tea bag and sugar in it, so he just needed to add the water. He had also made himself a bacon sandwich which he took to the kitchen table with his cup of tea and he started to eat his breakfast.

While he ate his breakfast he was reading the morning newspaper. On the front page was a story about the pocket watch killer. With the story there was a photograph. The photo was of a woodland area and all the stranger could see at first were the trees. But then he spotted something else within the photo. The more he looked at the photo the more obvious it became. What he could actually see was a person. The stranger was wondering if the person who took the photo had actually caught the killer on film. Now, the stranger wanted to go for a look during the day more than ever. When he had finished his breakfast and had his shoes and coat on he made his way to the area again.

As he was doing that O'Brien was in the tree house. O'Brien was now a little fed up with being in the tree house and had decided to go elsewhere today. When he was happy that his bags were packed and he hadn't forgotten anything he started to make a move. Before he made his way down he had a real good look around to make sure that no one was in the area, then when he was happy, he made his way down.

O'Brien didn't want to go too far away from the centre of Cornwall because that is where he felt the most comfortable. For now he decided to head towards Truro. To go to Truro he had to start his journey by heading back towards the railway tracks. As he was making his way back towards the tracks the stranger was parking his car where he had parked it the previous evening. When he had turned off the engine he sat there for a little while. Then, he got out of the car and made his way to the railway tracks. The stranger was totally unaware that O'Brien was walking in his direction.

Before long, the stranger could see the train tracks. When he reached the tracks he paused and looked both ways to make sure there wasn't a train coming. When he was happy that nothing was coming he began to cross the tracks. As he did so he noticed something. As he looked he could see some movement within the trees on the opposite side. As he looked more closely he could just about make out a person. The first thought that came to the stranger was that it could be the killer that was walking towards him. Just in case it was O'Brien, the stranger decided to get out of sight.

Along the path the stranger had just walked down was lined with trees, so he went back along the path and hid amongst the trees. From where he was hiding he could still see the train tracks. Just then, he saw someone on the other side of the tracks. On the news he had watched the previous evening they showed a photo of O'Brien, and he was sure that the person he was looking at was O'Brien. When O'Brien was happy that a train wasn't coming he crossed the tracks and made his way down the path.

When O'Brien was far enough down the path the stranger came out of hiding and started to follow him. The stranger was being extra careful because he didn't want to be seen by O'Brien. Every so often O'Brien would look behind him and the stranger would have to duck out of sight so that he wouldn't be seen. One time when O'Brien looked around the stranger was a little slow in getting out of sight and was almost seen by O'Brien.

As they were about to come off the path a police car suddenly came into sight and stopped dead. At the sight of the police car O'Brien also stopped in his tracks. When O'Brien stopped the stranger had to stop too. O'Brien didn't want to be seen by the police so he very quickly got out of sight. To his right there was a large tree and he hid behind it but so that he could still see the police car. The stranger too got out of sight because he didn't want to be by O'Brien or the police.

"They know you're here," said the voice.

O'Brien ignored the voice and continued to watch the police car. As the police car was parked the officer in the passenger seat got out of the car. The officer appeared to be stretching his legs while he had the chance. Just then, a voice could be heard coming over the police radio, at which point the officer got back into the car and closed the door. After another moment or so the police set off again.

"You were lucky this time, be more careful," said the voice.

O'Brien waited a minute or so for the police car to leave the area. Then, he slowly began to come out from behind the tree he was hiding behind. He stood there and looked for a moment, just to make sure the police car wasn't coming back. When he was happy that it wasn't coming back, he slowly made his way to the end of the path, where again he paused for a moment. Before he came off the path he wanted to make sure that no one was around, especially the police. When he was happy that he couldn't see anyone, O'Brien set off. All the while the stranger was still following him.

As O'Brien was making his way to Truro with the stranger following, Jordan was in her room at the bed and breakfast. Jordan was thinking about O'Brien and was wondering where he was. She knew that she had to be out looking for him and she was deciding where to go first. Something was telling her to go to the caravan park, the caravan park where O'Brien had his static caravan. When she was ready Jordan went to the room next door to hers to get Jarvis. Soon, the two of them were walking down to the car.

"So, where are we off to this morning?" said Jarvis.

"We're going to the caravan park," said Jordan.

"The one that O'Brien has a static caravan on?"

"Yes."

"Why are we going there?"

"I don't quite know, something is telling me that we need to go there."

"You never know, O'Brien may be stupid enough to return there," said Jarvis.

Jordan wasn't really in a talkative mood so the journey to the caravan park was in silence. Jarvis didn't really mind because he knew that Jordan was thinking about the case. Plus it gave him the opportunity to look around at the beautiful views of Cornwall. As he was looking around Jarvis was sure that he saw O'Brien.

"Pull over and stop as soon as you can," said Jarvis.

"Why, what's up?" said Jordan.

"I think I've just seen O'Brien."

The first chance she got Jordan pulled over and stopped the car. When the car was at a standstill the two of them got out of the car and started to look for who Jarvis thought was O'Brien.

"Where is he?" said Jordan.

"Just down there on our side of the road walking away from us. The one carrying a few bags," said Jarvis.

"Yes, I see him. You stay with the car because I may need you to come and get me."

At that, she gave him the car keys and set off after who the man. Jordan needed to get close enough to this person so see if it was O'Brien. This person was now a fair way in front of Jordan and she had to hurry to catch up with him. There were quite a lot of people out and about today and every so often Jordan would lose sight of the person that she was following.

Just a little way away there was a beach and it appeared that this person was heading towards it. Before they reached the beach the person that Jordan was following went into a shop. When she arrived at the shop Jordan could see the person through the shop window, so she decided to watch him from the street for now instead of going inside. From where she was stood Jordan still couldn't see whether this person was O'Brien because he had his back to her.

As she was stood there a loud crashing sound came from her left. When she looked Jordan could see a metal stand with newspapers and magazines had been accidentally knocked over. When Jordan looked back towards the shop she couldn't see the person that she was following any more. So, she went into the shop and had a real good look around, but she couldn't see him anywhere. She went back onto the street and had a good look around. When she couldn't see him anywhere Jordan realised that he must have snook out of the shop when she was distracted by the paper stand. At that, she went back to the car to continue the journey to the caravan park.

Jordan and Jarvis continued their journey to the caravan park. As they travelled Jordan couldn't help but think about the person that she had just followed. She was wondering if it was O'Brien or not.

Soon, they were at the caravan park. Jordan found a spot to park her car so that she had a clear view of O'Brien caravan. While they were sat there Jarvis began to feel the call of nature.

"I need to go to the toilet. Caravan parks usually have public toilets so I'll go and have a look," said Jarvis.

"Okay," said Jordan.

Jarvis got out of the car to go and look for the toilets. For a moment or so Jordan watched him walk away. When he was out of sight Jordan's attention went back to O'Brien's caravan. She began to wonder if Jarvis was right and O'Brien was stupid enough to return to his caravan. In her career as a police officer and then as a private investigator she had known criminals to do some stupid things.

Before long Jarvis had found the public toilets. He went into one of the cubicles, closed the cubicle door behind him and proceeded to use the toilet. Very shortly, Jarvis heard someone else enter the toilets. At first, he didn't think anything of it but he could hear this person moving around and then talking. At first, Jarvis didn't bother to listen to the person because he thought they were talking to someone on their mobile phone. As Jarvis was still in the cubicle the person was still unaware that Jarvis was even there.

As Jarvis was finishing and was about to come out of the cubicle, he heard the person say two words that really got him interested. Those words were pocket watch. Now, Jarvis knew that he had to get hold of Jordan, so he pulled out his mobile phone. Jarvis knew if he called Jordan he would be heard, so he texted her instead. In the text he told her that he could be on to something and asked her if she could come around to the toilets as quickly as she could.

When Jordan received the text message she was in a little world of her own and the sound of her phone going off made her jump a little. When she looked at her phone, she saw that it was a text off Jarvis.

"Don't tell me, you've got lost," said Jordan.

Then, Jordan saw the message. When she had finished reading, she suddenly became really curious. She made her way around to the toilets. At first, Jordan didn't know where the toilets were so she started by going the same direction as Jarvis. Before long the toilet building came in to view and Jordan started to walk towards them. As she did so a man came walking out of the gents, then, a moment or so later Jarvis came walking out. When Jordan saw Jarvis, she walked towards him.

"What's going on?" Jordan asked.

"When I was in the cubicle that guy came into the toilet block. At first, I didn't think anything of it, but then I heard him talking. While he was talking, I heard him say the words 'pocket watch'. At that point, I opened the cubicle door slightly, at which point I saw him talking on his mobile. Then I texted you," said Jarvis.

This really piqued Jordan's interest. Jordan asked Jarvis to go back to the car as she was going to see where this new lead was going to take her.

"What about O'Brien's caravan?" said Jarvis.

"You keep an eye on it and I'll call you when I need you," said Jordan.

As they were walking both Jordan and Jarvis could see this person was heading in the direction of O'Brien's caravan. For the time being the two of them kept their distance so they could see exactly what he was up to. As they got level with O'Brien's caravan the person they were following stopped and gave it a real good look. As he did that Jordan and Jarvis didn't want to make it obvious that they were watching him, so they walked straight to the car and got in and sat there for a moment. They glanced over to O'Brien's caravan, but could see the man was still standing there looking at the caravan.

"I wonder what he's up to?" said Jarvis.

"I don't know," said Jordan.

As they were watching him, he walked away from the caravan and went and sat on a nearby bench. Now, Jordan was pleased that she decided to return to the caravan park because she could have stumbled onto another lead.

At this time O'Brien was still making his way to Truro. The stranger, the one that Jordan had noticed, was still following O'Brien. The stranger was by now becoming a little fed up and bored with following O'Brien. He also realised that he was quite a way away from his car. Also, he didn't want O'Brien to see him. So, he made the decision to go back to his car. At one point, as he was walking back to his car the stranger looked back and he saw O'Brien walking away in the distance.

While he was walking O'Brien was thinking about exactly where he wanted to go. He was debating whether to go to his caravan or not. He hadn't been there for a good while and he was thinking that the police might not have anyone watching it any longer. The more he thought about it the more he thought it was a good idea. He also knew that he needed a shower and he could also wash his clothes. With this in mind he decided that he would make his way back to his caravan.

While O'Brien was making his way back to his caravan, DS Mike Lucas was having a drive around. Lucas was really becoming fed up with this case now. He really wanted to catch O'Brien and have him put in prison where he belonged. Lucas was having a drive around in the hope that he would get a glimpse of O'Brien. Lucas was driving around the areas where O'Brien's victims were found, knowing that serial killers liked to re-visit their crime scenes.

But after almost two hours of driving around Lucas had visited all the crime scenes. He didn't want to go back to the station just yet so he was thinking where to go next. As he was driving, he saw David Crammer walking towards him with a large bag hanging off his left shoulder.

"I wonder what you are up to," Lucas thought to himself.

The first chance he got Lucas stopped his car, turned around and went to catch up with Crammer. But when Lucas reached the spot where he'd seen Crammer, he couldn't see him any more. So, he drove slowly down the road looking for him.

"Where have you gone?" Lucas said to himself.

Just then, he spotted Crammer going into a café. The first chance he got Lucas parked his car. When he arrived at the café Lucas didn't go in because he didn't want Crammer to know that he had seen him. There were some tables and chairs outside the café so Lucas sat down at one of the tables. From where he was sat, he could see that Crammer was sat at a table with a couple of people. One of the people Lucas could see was Joe Crammer, David's brother, but he couldn't quite see who the other person was. He couldn't even tell if the other person was male or female.

As they were sat there someone from the café brought over what appeared to be hot drinks for the three of them.

At this point, Lucas would give anything to be able to listen to what they were talking about. Lucas knew that he was looking at O'Brien for the murders but he couldn't help but think that the Crammer brothers were involved somehow.

While Lucas was watching the three of them, Jordan and Jarvis were still at the caravan park. They were still watching the person they had come across. As they watched him, he kept looking over to O'Brien's caravan. At this point, he went over to the caravan and tried the door handle. When he saw that it was locked, he went back to the bench again and sat down. Jordan was beginning to wonder if he was a colleague of Lucas who was keeping an eye on the caravan just in case O'Brien returned. But if that was the case, Jordan thought, then where was his car. All the while O'Brien was getting closer and closer to the caravan park.

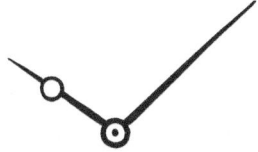

CHAPTER FIFTEEN

O'Brien was about half a mile away from the caravan park. His caravan was near the front entrance and he was approaching the caravan park's rear entrance. As he was getting closer the voice started to talk to him.

"You're doing the wrong thing. If you go through with this you'll be caught and put in jail, is that what you want? How do you know that there isn't someone there waiting for you to make this mistake?" said the voice.

For a moment, O'Brien slowed down to consider what the voice had said. On this occasion the voice made some sense. As he was thinking about it, O'Brien realised that he didn't have to go to his caravan for a shower or to wash his clothes because not too far from the rear entrance there was a shower block that anyone on the caravan park could use. Also, a little further round from the shower block was a small launderette where he could wash his clothes.

Soon, O'Brien had the rear entrance to the caravan park in his sights. As he approached the entrance O'Brien slowed right down. He didn't know if the police were still on the caravan park waiting for him to return. Just outside the entrance he had a real good look up and down the road but couldn't see any police. For a moment or so he stood there plucking up the courage to go in. Before he walked through the entrance to see if there were any police he just peered round the wall of the entrance, but he couldn't see anyone. When he was comfortable, he walked through the entrance and made his way straight to the launderette. When he arrived at the launderette, he was confident that he hadn't been seen.

Luckily for O'Brien the launderette didn't have a member of staff during the day. With no one else using the launderette, O'Brien felt quite comfortable. He very quickly took his dirty clothes out of his bag and put them in one of the washing machines. He had some washing powder with him, so, when he had put the washing powder in the machine and the door was closed, he put the right money in, which started the washer automatically. When he was happy the machine was working okay, O'Brien grabbed his towel, soap, shampoo and went for a shower. Before he left the launderette, he had a good look around outside to make sure there was no one about. When he was happy that no one was walking nearby, O'Brien made his way to the shower block.

Within twenty minutes O'Brien had finished his shower and he was dressed again. When he was ready and he had his towel along with his soap and shampoo, he made his way back to the launderette. When he was about to walk out of the shower block, O'Brien peered through the door to see if there was anyone around, but there wasn't. At that, he made his way back to the launderette. When he was back, he could see the washing machine with his clothes in was about halfway through its wash cycle.

While he waited for the washing machine to finish washing his clothes, O'Brien went as far as he could to the back of the launderette, to reduce the chances of him being seen by anyone who passed. When he was at the back near the dryers, he saw that there was a door leading to a small room. So, he went into the room to hide for a while.

"You should be safe in here for now," said the voice.

While he was in the room, he saw a small table with a chair next to it. As he waited for the washer to finish, he went and sat down. While he was sat there, he listened to the washer wash his clothes and prayed that no one came in to use the launderette. After a few minutes of sitting there O'Brien could hear voices. When he listened more closely, he could tell they were coming from just outside the front door of the launderette. O'Brien was nervous about anyone coming in and seeing him, so, he went to have a look at who it was and to see where they were. When he peered around the door, he could see two women who appeared to be out walking their dogs. The two women were stood just a few feet from the door, having a chat. While O'Brien was watching them one of the women came to put something in the bin, which was just outside the launderette. As she did this O'Brien held his breath; his heart felt like it could stop at any moment. When she had put her rubbish in the bin, she glanced into the launderette for a few seconds. Then, she went back to the other woman and the two of them carried on with their walk.

"You were really lucky there. You need to get out of here as soon as you can," said the voice.

Before O'Brien realised it, the washer had finished and he was putting his clothes into one of the driers. When he had set the dryer going, he went and sat down in the back room again. Up to now, apart from the two women no one had been anywhere near the launderette. When he had been in the back room for about fifteen minutes, O'Brien suddenly got the urge to have a walk round to his caravan. He wanted to see if anyone was watching it.

"Going around to your caravan is a stupid idea, someone is bound to see you," said the voice.

For a moment or so O'Brien stayed in the back room of the launderette and thought about what the voice had just said. He wondered if it would be a good idea or not. But curiosity got the better of him and he started to make his way round to his caravan. Before he left the back room, he glanced through the door to see if there was anyone in the launderette or outside. He couldn't see anyone so he made his way to the front door. When he was at the front door, he had a look around to make sure that there wasn't anyone out and about. When he was happy that no one was around he left the launderette and made his way to his caravan.

"This is a very bad idea," said the voice.

O'Brien ignored the voice and continued on his way to his caravan. While he was making his way round to his caravan, O'Brien's eyes were everywhere. Every slight movement and every sound he checked to see what it was. When he was just about halfway round to his caravan a door to another caravan began to open. As O'Brien watched the door open, he froze on the spot and for a moment he didn't know what to do.

"I told you that this was a bad idea," said the voice.

As the caravan door opened the person who lived there started to come out. But when they were halfway through the door they turned around and went back in. It was as if they had forgotten something. Luckily for O'Brien the person never saw him. While the person was inside their caravan O'Brien took the chance to get past the caravan.

"Once again, you've been very lucky. You have been pushing your luck recently," said the voice.

Now, O'Brien's attention was on his own caravan. He was so curious to see if anyone was still watching it or not.

O'Brien now had to go around one more corner and his caravan would be in full view. O'Brien didn't want to take the chance of being seen if there was someone there watching his caravan. Just before he went around the corner there was another caravan. So, he went over to it and walked along it. When he was at the end, he peered round and looked towards his own caravan. As he looked past his caravan, he saw the car with Jordan and Jarvis sat in it.

"That's the private investigator that is looking for you and she is watching your caravan. I told you that this was a bad idea," said the voice.

As he looked past Jordan's car, O'Brien saw someone sat on the bench. He too appeared to be watching his caravan.

"I wonder who he could be and why is he interested in your caravan," said the voice.

O'Brien was really curious about the person who was sat on the bench. He didn't seem to think that he was a police officer, but he could be mistaken. Just then, O'Brien heard someone to his right hand side.

"Hey you, what are you doing there?"

When O'Brien looked, he saw someone stood in the doorway of their caravan looking at him. At the same time Jordan, Jarvis and the man sat on the bench looked in his direction. As they did so O'Brien was moving away and they only saw his shoulder and arm.

"I wonder who that was?" said Jarvis.

"I don't know, but it might be worth going for a look," said Jordan.

At that, the two of them got out of the car and went for a look. As they were doing that O'Brien was racing to the launderette.

As Jordan and Jarvis went to see who the disappearing person was, the man who was sat on the bench, out of curiosity, followed them to see what was going on. When Jordan and Jarvis reached the caravan where they saw the person disappearing and went around the side of it, they couldn't see anyone. They both knew whoever it was couldn't just have disappeared into thin air, so, they carried on to see if they could find out who it was. O'Brien knew a way to get to the launderette that reduced the chances of being seen and he was almost at the launderette.

When O'Brien got into the launderette, he saw that the dryer was still going. He went straight over to the dryer, opened the door and started to take out his clothes. As he did so he could feel that they were almost dry. He put all of his clothes back in the bag and then he zipped up the bag. He didn't even bother to fold his clothes.

When he was ready to leave O'Brien looked out of the window at the front of the launderette to see if anyone was coming, but he couldn't see anyone. At that, he grabbed all of his belongings and made his way out of the launderette.

Before he left the building, he had one last look to make sure no one was coming, but he couldn't see anyone. So, he left the launderette and made his way off the caravan park as quickly as he could. As O'Brien came level with the shower block, Jordan and Jarvis were walking down the path and saw him.

"Is that O'Brien?" said Jordan.

"Yes, it is," said Jarvis.

"Here are the car keys. You go and get the car while I follow O'Brien," said Jordan.

"Are you sure about that?"

"Yes, I am. Go and get the car and hurry."

As Jarvis turned around to go back to the car, he saw the man from the bench about twenty feet away. He appeared to be watching what he and Jordan were doing. As Jarvis passed the man, he tried to make it look like he wasn't watching them, which made Jarvis a little more suspicious. Jarvis didn't want to leave Jordan any longer than necessary following O'Brien by herself, so, he forgot about the man and hurried back to the car.

As Jarvis was getting back to the car as quickly as he could Jordan was keeping up with O'Brien. She wasn't getting too close to him because she didn't want to be seen by him.

O'Brien didn't want to go anywhere there were a lot of people, so he went in the general area of the railway tracks. He wasn't going to the same place as before but he knew that there were a few quiet places around there for him to hide.

O'Brien was moving at such a brisk pace Jordan was having difficulty in keeping up with him, but she was determined not to let him get away. While she was following O'Brien, Jordan realised that Lucas would want to know what was happening. Lucas was still sat outside the café watching Crammer when his mobile started to ring.

"Hello," said Lucas.

"Hi Lucas, it's Jordan. I thought that you would want to know that I've found O'Brien and I'm following him now," said Jordan.

"Where are you?"

Jordan told him where they were and where they were heading. When they hung up Lucas looked in the café at Crammer. He really wanted to know what he was up to, but it was O'Brien that they were after. So, Lucas went back to his car and made his way to Jordan's location as quickly as he could. Lucas knew that this was probably the closest he had come to catching O'Brien.

Meanwhile, Jordan was still close to O'Brien. Now, O'Brien was leading her away from the busier areas and into a more secluded area. At this point, Jordan was beginning to wish that Lucas would hurry up. Where they were was somewhere that Jordan had never been before. The place they were walking through had fields all around them. To the right Jordan could see some houses dotted around in the distance. In the front of them and to the left slightly were some trees. O'Brien appeared to be heading towards them.

Jordan realised while she was following him O'Brien was looking everywhere other than behind him. If he had done so he would have, without fail, seen Jordan.

Soon, O'Brien was at the trees. Jordan watched him walk to the treeline, then disappear within the trees. When she reached the treeline Jordan hesitated for a moment. She was wondering if following O'Brien into the trees would be a good idea or not. As she stood there peering through the trees Jordan could see O'Brien disappearing into the distance. Just then, Jordan received a text message. When she looked at it, she could see that it was from Lucas asking her where she was. She very quickly replied with her location. Then, she continued to watch O'Brien walk away from her. She knew if she didn't do anything, she would end up losing him.

"To hell with this," Jordan said to herself.

Jordan entered the trees and continued her chase of O'Brien. Jordan then received a text message from Lucas saying that he was on his way and for her not to enter the trees until he got there, but it was already too late.

Jordan could just about see O'Brien in the distance weaving his way through the trees. She was determined not to lose him. Every so often, she would lose sight of him because of the trees but she soon found him again. Just then, Jordan received another text message.

"I'm in the field next to some trees, where are you?" said Lucas.

"I'm within the trees following O'Brien," Jordan replied.

"She couldn't wait," Lucas said to himself.

He then made his way within the trees to catch up with Jordan. As Lucas was making his way through the trees Jordan put her phone away to continue to follow O'Brien. As she looked up, she realised that she had lost sight of O'Brien.

"Christ, that's the last thing I need," Jordan said to herself.

What she decided to do was to go in the direction she'd last seen him, but she did so very carefully. As she approached the section of trees where she last saw O'Brien, her eyes were everywhere. With not spotting him at all, she began to wonder if he was laying low somewhere. Within the trees there were plenty of places for O'Brien to hide. The grass was long, there were large bushes everywhere and there were the trees themselves.

As she slowly walked through the trees Jordan suddenly heard something and she stopped in her tracks. As she stood there, she heard the sound again. She couldn't see anything and couldn't quite tell where the sound was coming from. As she looked behind her and to her left slightly Jordan could see Lucas walking towards her. She knew that he was too far away to have made the sound that she had heard. When Lucas looked at Jordan, she put her finger to her lips telling him to keep quiet. Within thirty seconds Lucas was stood next to Jordan.

"So, where is he?" whispered Lucas.

"I last saw him when I sent you the text, then, when I looked up, he was gone. But I'm sure he is hiding out around here somewhere," whispered Jordan.

At that, the two of them continued the search for O'Brien. Little did they know but O'Brien was about fifty feet away and he was watching them. He was hiding within some very long thick grass but he was able to peer out and watch what they were doing. Both Jordan and Lucas were walking in the general direction of where O'Brien was but slightly to the left of his position. The more they walked the nearer to O'Brien's position they were getting. When they arrived at the long grass the two of them were about twenty feet from where O'Brien was hiding. They too stood there looking over the long grass while deciding what to do next.

"I think it would be a good idea to have a few officers here to help us to search through this grass!" said Lucas.

At that, Lucas called the station and asked for some officers to join them at their location to help them with the search for O'Brien. From where he was positioned O'Brien could just about hear Lucas asking the station for some officers to assist them in their search for him. Now, O'Brien had to work out how he was going to get out of there without being seen. He began to look around to see if there was a discreet way out. As he looked around, he moved some of the long grass and Jordan noticed.

"Did you see that?" said Jordan.

"See what?" said Lucas.

"Some of the long grass over there moved a far bit. What's the betting that it's O'Brien?"

"They've noticed where you are. You're going to have to be really careful now," said the voice.

O'Brien knew that he had to keep still now, but he also knew that he had to get out of there and sooner rather than later. As he peered through the long grass O'Brien could see Jordan looking directly where he was hiding.

O'Brien grabbed his bags in readiness to run, but something made him stay where he was. He knew if he made a run for it now Jordan and Lucas would spot him and give chase. O'Brien was hoping that Jordan and Lucas would look the other way so that he could make off.

"What are you waiting for, you know that others are coming. You'll have a better chance of getting away with only two of them," said the voice.

O'Brien was really eager to get going but Jordan was still looking right at where he was hiding. Jordan was still as sure as she could be that O'Brien was hiding directly where she was looking. Not being the kind just to stand around doing nothing, Jordan started to walk through the long grass towards the spot. As she did so, Lucas grabbed her by the arm.

"Where do you think you're going?" said Lucas.

"I'm not hanging around waiting for your men to arrive. I need to get in there and find O'Brien," said Jordan.

At that, she broke free from Lucas's grasp and walked towards where she thought O'Brien was hiding. For a moment Lucas watched her walk away from him. He knew that he couldn't leave her on her own to find a serial killer by herself, so he started to follow her. As he did so he heard someone call out his name. When he turned towards the sound of the voice, he saw that it was the back up that he had asked for. At that, Lucas started to make his way towards the officers. When he had walked only a few feet he heard Jordan call out. When he turned back around, he saw O'Brien running with Jordan giving chase. Lucas immediately gave the order to the other officers to help give chase.

Even though O'Brien was still carrying all of his bags he was somehow managing to make it difficult for Jordan and the police to catch him. As they were running Jordan could see a very large bush about twenty feet in front of them. When he reached it O'Brien disappeared behind it, but a few seconds later when the Jordan and the police arrived on the other side of the bush O'Brien was nowhere to be seen. At that, they all stopped and looked around for O'Brien. After a moment or so they all started to walk forward in search of O'Brien, with Jordan leading the way. As Jordan was looking around for O'Brien, she could see that they were in a quite a large field. Also, she noticed that the officers that were with her were going to different parts of the field to look for O'Brien.

"How could you hide so quickly?" Jordan said to herself.

Then, it dawned on her. With O'Brien getting out of sight so quickly he must be somewhere near the bush. So, Jordan turned around and slowly made her back towards the large bush. While she was walking towards the bush Jordan couldn't really see anywhere for someone to hide, but she knew that O'Brien had to be somewhere. When she reached the bush, she started to check it over for any possible hiding places. As she did so Lucas finally arrived at the location. When he saw Jordan checking out the bush, he went over to her.

"What's happened?" said Lucas.

"We chased O'Brien to this area, then he appeared to just disappear," said Jordan.

"What are you doing here, then?"

"O'Brien didn't have much time to get out of sight before all of us came to this side of the bush. So, I'm thinking that he will be hiding somewhere within or near the bush."

"Makes sense."

Jordan and Lucas could see some houses and a road not far away. They couldn't see O'Brien on the street anywhere so it made sense that O'Brien was close by. Lucas then started to help Jordan look for O'Brien's hiding place. As he did so the two of them heard one of the officers cry out. When they turned around, they saw someone running and carrying bags with the other officers chasing them. Instantly they assumed it was O'Brien and the two of them started to give chase. Very soon this person was caught and brought to the ground. When Jordan and Lucas arrived at the scene an officer and this person were picking themselves off the floor. But straight away they could see that it wasn't O'Brien.

"Who the hell are you?" said Jordan.

"Steve Mills, I was just running for my bus."

"This isn't O'Brien, let him go," said Lucas.

O'Brien was actually hiding in the bush and he was watching what was going on. While Jordan and the police's attention were on this other person, he took the opportunity to sneak away. Jordan, Lucas and the other officers had another look around the area for O'Brien, but deep down they all knew that he would be long gone by now. After another half an hour of looking the search was called off and they all left the area.

"You were lucky this time," said the voice.

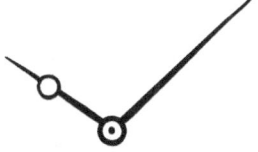

CHAPTER SIXTEEN

———

W hen Jordan was back at the car with Jarvis, she had a chat with Lucas. The two of them basically agreed to continue to keep each other informed about the case.

When they were in the car Jordan allowed Jarvis to drive because she wanted to think about what had just happened. Jordan wanted to go back to the bed and breakfast so she asked Jarvis to take her back there.

On the journey back to the bed and breakfast Jordan was really quiet. She knew how close they were to catching O'Brien and she was really angry with herself for not getting him. Jordan was beginning to wonder where O'Brien was going. Deep down she felt that wherever he was heading it wouldn't be too far away.

Whilst waiting at a set of traffic lights Jordan glanced out of the door window. As she looked towards the bus stop that was nearby, she recognised someone who was standing there. As she was about to get out of the car the lights changed to green and Jarvis started to go.

"Pull over as soon as you can," said Jordan.

"Why, have you seen something?" said Jarvis.

"I've seen someone that I would like to talk to," said Jordan.

There was a street just coming up on the left and Jarvis turned down it. When the car was parked and had come to a stop Jordan got out of the car and went to talk the person at the bus stop. Out of curiosity Jarvis also went to see who this person was.

When they were back on the main road Jordan could see the person that she wanted to talk to was still stood at the bus stop. As they were walking down the road Jarvis was trying to work out who Jordan wanted to talk to.

"Ahh, it's the stranger that you've noticed," said Jarvis.

"Yes, I want to find out what he knows about the case," said Jordan.

As they approached the stranger his mobile phone started to ring. As he went to his pocket to pull out his phone, he saw Jordan walking towards him. When he answered the phone, the stranger told the person on the other end that he would call them back. Then, he hung up and put the phone back in to his pocket.

"I wondered when you would catch up with me," said the stranger.

"Yes, I've been trying to talk to you for a while now about the murders in the area. I'm curious to hear what you know about them," said Jordan.

"What makes you think that I know anything about them?"

"Are you telling me that you don't?" said Jordan.

For a moment or two the stranger just stood there and looked at Jordan. She could tell that he was thinking about her question. As the stranger was thinking Jordan could see a bus coming towards the bus stop that they were stood at. She began to wonder what the stranger would do once the bus arrived.

"Well, are you going to answer my question?" said Jordan.

"If you insist," said the stranger. "I don't know anything about the actual murders other than what I have read in the papers or seen on the news, but I do know Mike O'Brien. Once, I lived on the same caravan park as him. His behaviour used to creep me out, so I found somewhere else to live. When the murders hit the news and that the police were looking for someone from a nearby caravan park I began to wonder if Mike had anything to do with it. So, I started to look into it. When you started to look into it, I overheard you say that you were a PI, so I followed you around to find out what you would uncover."

"What do you mean when you said that O'Brien's behaviour used to creep you out?" said Jordan.

"On the rare occasion I talked to him he told me once that he had some kind of mental illness and he was on medication to help control the illness. Sometimes I swear his behaviour was really weird."

"What do you mean weird?" said Jordan.

"It was as if he was off his medication and his mind was going a little manic to say the least," said the stranger.

"Okay, that's about all that I can think of asking you for now, other than to ask what your name is?" said Jordan.

"I'd rather not say."

Jordan wasn't a police officer any more so she couldn't make him tell her. The bus that Jordan saw coming had already left, so she asked the stranger if he wanted a lift anywhere but he said that he would be alright and that he would wait for the next bus. At that, both Jordan and Jarvis made their way back to the car.

"What do you think, do you believe him?" said Jarvis.

"Yes, I do. But I feel that he's missing something out," said Jordan.

"What do you think that could be?"

"I'm unsure, but I will find out what it is sooner or later."

While Jordan and Jarvis were making their way back to the car Mark Barker, the journalist, was in his car having a drive around. As he was driving around Mark saw David Crammer waiting on a street corner. Mark knew that David was an ex-con because he'd written a story on David's previous crime.

"What are you up to?" Mark said to himself.

The first chance he got Mark pulled over and parked his car. When he was parked, he grabbed his mobile phone. Also, he picked up and put into his jacket pocket a small digital camera that he had with him. When he was ready, he got out of his car and went to see what David was up to, making sure his car was locked before he left it.

Very quickly Mark was back where he had seen David. He didn't want to be seen by David, so Mark looked for a place where he could be out of sight but still able to keep an eye on him. Mark saw a post box that was just in front of a small, low wall. He was on the side of the post box that would block him from David's view, so he went and sat on the wall. Every so often Mark would glance round the post box to check on what David was doing. David kept looking up and down the street, then, he would check his watch. It was as if he was waiting for someone.

When Mark had been sat there for a few minutes David received a call on his mobile. Mark could hear David talking on the phone but he couldn't quite tell what he was saying. While Mark was peering round the post box trying to hear what was being said David started to walk in his direction. When he saw David walking in his direction Mark took out his phone from his jacket pocket and pretended to be writing a text. When David had walked by and was far enough away Mark put his phone away and started to follow him.

The little bit of the conversation that Mark overheard made it sound like David was going to meet someone. Mark tried to get a little closer so that he could hear some more of the conversation. Mark had wondered for a while if David had anything to do with Mike O'Brien, the main suspect in the case. Just when he got close enough to hear what was being said, David ended the call then put his phone in his jacket pocket. Mark was still curious to know where David was going, so, he continued to follow him.

As Mark was following David, Jordan and Jarvis were arriving back at the bed and breakfast. Jordan was still really frustrated about coming so close to catching O'Brien. Jarvis saw how frustrated she was. He knew when she was like this, she preferred to be alone, so he went back to his own room. When he was in his room and had taken off his coat Jarvis sat in the chair that was next to the window. The chair was positioned so Jarvis could look out of the window. While he was sat there, he started to think about the case. He began to think where O'Brien could have possibly gone. With him being a retired criminologist

Jarvis knew that a serial killer will not stop until someone makes them stop.

While he was sat there, he could hear something just outside of his room. At first, Jarvis didn't really think anything of it. Just then, there was something pushed under his door. Out of curiosity he walked across to see what it was. When he got to the door and looked down, he saw that it was an envelope. He picked it up and then opened the door. When he looked out there wasn't anyone there. When he looked up and down the hall, he still couldn't see anyone, so he went back in to his room. Jarvis looked at the envelope. He saw that there wasn't anything written on the front of it. So, out of curiosity Jarvis opened the envelope to see what was inside. When the envelope was open and he pulled the contents, Jarvis saw that it was a note. The note said: "If you want to know more about the pocket watch killer then come to The Dog and Partridge pub in Truro and come alone!"

The first thing that Jarvis thought was that this was a little weird. He was about to go to Jordan's room to tell her about the note but there was something stopping him. Jarvis was beginning to wonder if he went it could go a long way to helping Jordan solve the case, but he wasn't sure what to do. Then, he made a decision.

"Just sitting here isn't going to get things done," Jarvis said to himself.

At that, he put on his shoes and coat and made his way to the Dog and Partridge. As he left the room, he closed the door as quietly as he could so that Jordan wouldn't hear. Then, he crept past Jordan's room. He then went downstairs and made his way out of the bed and breakfast. A little way down from the bed and breakfast was a taxi rank where Jarvis was able to take a taxi to the Dog and Partridge.

As Jarvis was sat in the taxi on the journey to Truro, he was thinking about the person he was going to meet. He was curious to know who it was. He couldn't imagine it being O'Brien but he was sure that it must be someone connected with the case somehow. As he was sat there thinking, he was totally unaware that there was a car following his taxi. He was actually being followed by the person who had pushed the note under his door back at the bed and breakfast.

Before long the taxi was pulling up outside the Dog and Partridge pub. Jarvis paid the driver, got out of the taxi and went in to the pub. When he was inside, he took a moment to have a look around. He wanted to see if he could recognise anyone. When he had a good look around Jarvis walked over to the bar and ordered himself a drink. When he received his drink and had paid for it, Jarvis sat on the vacant bar stool. As he was sat there, he had a real good look around. Jarvis could see customers eating meals, drinking drinks and talking amongst themselves. But what he was really interested in was the person who had asked him here in the first place. As he was sat there looking around, the barman who has served him returned with Jarvis's change and handed over a piece of paper.

"I've been asked to give you this," said the barman.

The note said: "Go and sit at the table right of the fire." So, Jarvis picked up his drink and did what the note asked of him. While he waited, he had a look around to see if there was anyone he recognised. Just then, he heard someone speak just behind him.

"Don't turn around," said a woman's voice.

"Who are you?" said Jarvis.

"Never mind that, I have some information for you."

"Yeah, and what's that?"

"I know how you can catch O'Brien," said the woman.

"Really, how am I going to do that?"

"I know all of his hiding places."

"And how do you know about his hiding places?"

"That isn't important right now, but what is important is that I know."

"Why don't you tell all this to the police?" said Jarvis.

"Because I don't trust the police, it has to be you and your PI friend. I am leaving an envelope on my chair. Wait two minutes then turn around and get it," said the woman.

"Wait, how do we contact you?"

Jarvis didn't receive a reply, all he heard was silence. At that point, Jarvis waited a couple of minutes then he turned around. As he did so he looked on the chair that was directly behind and saw the envelope. Jarvis picked up the envelope and opened it. Inside was a list of places around Cornwall. After a few minutes of looking over the list Jarvis put the list back in to the envelope, took out his mobile phone from his jacket pocket and called for a taxi to take him back to the bed and breakfast. Jarvis then finished his drink and went outside to wait for the taxi.

Just outside the pub there was a seating area for the pub's customers to use. While he waited for his taxi to arrive Jarvis sat on one of the seats. A little way up the road, to the left from where Jarvis was sat, was a parked car. Sat in the driver's seat of the car was the woman who had just spoken to Jarvis. But Jarvis was totally unaware that he was being watched by the woman.

Just then, Jarvis's taxi arrived. Jarvis stood and walked over to the taxi, got in to the back seat and told the driver where he wanted to go. When the taxi set off the woman started her car and followed. On the journey back to the bed and breakfast Jarvis realised that it was the same taxi driver that had taken him to the Dog and Partridge. Jarvis noticed that the driver kept checking his mirrors.

"Is everything okay?" said Jarvis.

"I'm not sure," said the driver.

"What do you mean you're not sure?"

"The car that is behind us I'm sure is the one which followed us to the Dog and Partridge earlier."

At that, Jarvis turned around to have a look. He looked at the driver to see if he recognised them, but he didn't.

"Do you know the person that's driving?" said the taxi driver.

"No, I don't," said Jarvis.

Jarvis turned back around in his seat to face forward again. For the rest of the journey Jarvis wondered who the person could be. Then, it began to dawn on him that the person driving the car could be the woman he had just met in the pub.

When they arrived back at the bed and breakfast, Jarvis paid the driver then went inside. Jordan was standing outside his room and turned to look at him.

"Where have you been?" said Jordan.

"I've been to the Dog and Partridge pub in Truro."

"And what have you been there for?"

"Following a lead. If you come inside, I will tell you all about it," said Jarvis.

At that, the two of them went into Jarvis's room. Jarvis told Jordan everything, from when the note was pushed under the door to when he arrived back to the bed and breakfast. While Jarvis spoke, Jordan listened intently. They went through the list place by place, and for Jordan there was one place that stood out – it was right where they had lost O'Brien a little earlier. It was described on the list as some kind of small wooden shed sort of building. To Jordan it seemed too good to be true and so they had to go and have a look.

Jordan went to her room to get her car keys and Jarvis waited in the hallway. When she had her car keys Jordan couldn't get down to the car quickly enough and Jarvis struggled to keep up with her.

As they were driving Jordan started to get a tingling feeling all over her. It was the kind of feeling that she always got every time she came close to solving a case.

Before long they were in the area where they had lost O'Brien. They just needed to find a parking spot. Just then, someone in front of them pulled out of a space on the side of the road and Jordan took the opportunity and pulled into that space. Then they made their way to the area where they had lost sight of O'Brien and began looking. When they were where Jordan had lost O'Brien they stated to look for a wooden shed kind of building. While they were walking around, they couldn't see a building of any kind, but after about fifteen minutes of looking Jarvis saw a small group of trees with what appeared to be a small building amongst them. Jarvis pointed it out to Jordan and the two of them went across to have a look.

As they approached the group of trees and the small building, they did so very carefully on the off chance that O'Brien was there. When they were level with the trees the two of them stopped and had a real good look at the building. They could tell that it was made out of wood and it was a small shed like building. What they couldn't work out was why it was there. After a couple of minutes of standing there they walked around the building to see if there were any windows for them to look through and see what it was like inside. The first side they walked down didn't have any windows, so they walked round to the back. There was a window but Jordan didn't want to be seen if there was anyone inside so, she stood to one side of the window and then she glanced in.

At first, she didn't spot anyone. While she had the chance, Jordan had a real good look around inside to see if anyone was using it to hide out there. At first, all she could see was what appeared to be some rusty old gardening tools. There didn't appear to be anyone hiding out there and she started to move away. As she did so she spotted something and she gave the item a real good look. Jordan could see it was a quite a large holdall with another one next to it.

"I think someone is hiding out here because there are a couple of large holdalls inside. Let's go round to the front to see if the door is unlocked," said Jordan.

At that, the two of them went round to the door. When they were at the door and Jordan tried to open it, they realised that it was locked. As they stood there thinking what to do next, they saw someone approaching the shed, but they couldn't quite see who it was. Straight away the two of them went down the side of the shed and got themselves out of sight. Within a few seconds of getting out of sight they heard someone unlock the shed door and go inside. After a moment the two of them made their way round to the door to see who it was. Jordan peered round the door frame to see who was inside. Straight away she knew who it was: it was David Crammer.

"What are you doing here?" said Jordan.

"Oh Christ, it's you," said David.

"Are you going to answer my question?"

"I don't want any more to do with this murder investigation so I've been hiding out here. What are you doing here?"

"We've been led to believe that O'Brien has been hiding out here, so we came to check it out," said Jordan.

"Well, he isn't here and he's never been here," said David.

At that, Mark Barker, the journalist, turned up at the shed. Jordan turned and looked at him with a glum face.

"What are you doing here?" said Jordan.

"Thought our friend David here was up to something, so I thought that I would follow him," said Mark.

"Well, I'm not. So, you can all go away and leave me alone!"

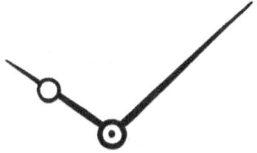

CHAPTER SEVENTEEN

As Jordan and Jarvis were at the shed talking to Mark Barker and David Crammer, O'Brien was in St Ives making his way to one of his hideouts.

"It may be an idea to get out of Cornwall all together," said the voice.

But O'Brien just ignored it. Where O'Brien was, was at an old abandoned scrap yard. The scrap yard had been abandoned for years and O'Brien knew that it would be unlikely that he would be disturbed. When he had used the scrap yard before to hide out, he never gained entry at the front entrance on the off chance that he may be seen by someone. Round the back was more hidden and there were a couple of places that O'Brien used to get in and out.

Behind the scrap yard there was a chain link fence which had a large hole in a couple of places which were about twenty feet apart from one another. Each hole was big enough for a person to fit through. Behind the scrap yard there was quite a large open space. There were other industrial buildings that were nearby but they weren't too close to the scrap yard. When O'Brien arrived at one of the holes in the fencing, he had a good look around to make sure that there was no one else was around to see him. When O'Brien was happy that nobody was around, he sneaked through the hole in the fence and made his way to the deserted office. When he was at the office door, he had another look around to make sure he wasn't seen by anyone. When he was happy that he hadn't been seen, he opened the unlocked door and made his way inside, closing the door behind him.

"Good job you got here without being seen," said the voice.

Now that he was in the office area O'Brien started to make himself comfortable. He began by taking his coat off and hanging it over one of the chairs that had been left behind. He placed his radio on a nearby desk and turned it on. The radio was tuned in to a local radio station. O'Brien mainly listened to the radio so that he could listen to the news, to be kept updated about his case and to find out what he could about the police activities.

When he had made himself comfortable, he realised that he was feeling hungry. So, he looked through his food supplies to see what he had. He saw that he several ready made sandwiches in plastic containers. So, he decided to have a couple of them. The sandwiches he chose were chicken and stuffing as well as a sausage and egg one.

As he sat there eating his sandwiches O'Brien was listening to his radio. As he listened the news came on. The main headline was about him and the murders. He sat there and listened intently. The news reader was updating the public on the police investigation, then went on to mention Jordan's name. At this point O'Brien became very upset and he threw the remainder of his second sandwich across the room. He then stood up and started to pace up and down the room.

"That PI has a lot to answer for," said the voice.

When O'Brien was this irate, he usually went looking for a victim. He knew that his belongings would be safe where they were so he went off to take out his frustrations. When he was out of the office, he closed the door and made it as secure as possible. When he was satisfied, he went out on the prowl. Jordan, DS Mike Lucas and the police in general had no idea of what was about to happen.

As O'Brien went out on the prowl Jordan and Jarvis were still at the first location on the list with David Crammer and Mark Barker. At this moment in time Jordan didn't have any interest in David and she wanted to go to the next location on the list, so she left him to it. As she walked away Mark walked with her and Jarvis.

"So, you have a new lead, then?" said Mark.

"Possibly," said Jordan.

"Any chance of you sharing?" said Mark.

"Not at present," said Jordan.

"Are you sure there's nothing that I can help you with?" said Mark.

"I'm positive, Jarvis and myself will be able to manage by ourselves, thank you," said Jordan.

At that, the three of them went their separate ways. Mark went back to his car with Jordan and Jarvis going to the next place on the list. By chance, the next place on the list was the scrap yard. When they were back at Jordan's car, they made their way to St Ives, where the scrap yard was. Luckily for the two of them the woman who gave Jarvis the list had written down directions on how to get to each place.

When they were in the car making their way to St Ives the two of them were unaware that they were being followed. The woman who had given Jarvis the list had decided to follow them to see if they would work their way through the list.

Soon, they were arriving in St Ives. All they had to do now was to find the scrap yard. The directions that the woman had given were quite specific. She had given very good landmarks to look out for and soon they were arriving at the scrap yard.

Jordan soon found a parking place and they were out of the car, looking for a way in. At the entrance to the scrap yard there were two large metal gates, so they went across to see if they were unlocked. As luck would have it the gates were unlocked. The gates were large, heavy dumpy things and it took the two of them to open the gates.

When the gates were open and the two of them had walked into the yard a little way, they stopped to have a look around the yard. They thought to themselves if O'Brien was in the yard he could be anywhere and they didn't want to walk into a trap, so they wanted to search the yard carefully. With the yard not being used for a few years there wasn't really much in it. There were five or six scrapped cars, several large pieces of scrap metal and a couple of large container units. One of the containers had been turned into an office.

After a moment or two of standing there looking around and not seeing anyone else there, Jordan and Jarvis started to walk around to see what else they could find. As they walked around the yard they always knew where one another was at all times. When they had walked around the yard and found nothing of interest, the two of them went over to the pair of containers.

They could see that one of them had been turned into an office. Jordan wanted to save the office until last so they started with the other container. Luckily for them when they tried the doors on the container they were unlocked and easy to open. When the doors were open, they could see what appeared to be surplus office furniture. There were some desks, chairs and filing cabinets. They looked inside the container just in case there was something of interest to the case, but after a few minutes they realised that there wasn't.

When they were ready the two of them walked round to the other container. With this container being turned into an office an ordinary door had been fitted into the side. Also, a couple of windows had been fitted to allow some light into the room. Before they even thought about trying to get into the office Jordan wanted to look through one of the windows to see if O'Brien was there or not. When she was at the window looking through, Jordan couldn't see O'Brien anywhere but she was able to get a real good look around the room. She could see that there wasn't much office furniture but she did notice some luggage. Jarvis was also looking through the window.

"I wonder if those are O'Brien's bags?" said Jordan.

"Could be," said Jarvis.

At that, Jordan went to see if the door was unlocked. She put her hand on the handle, turned it and pushed the door. As she did so the door opened. For a moment the two of them stood there and looked in. With O'Brien probably already being there and more and more likely going to return at some point, the two of them were a little nervous.

After a moment or so the two of them decided to go in for a closer look. At the moment, Jordan was only interested in taking a look at the bags. She opened one and started to slowly go through it. If these were O'Brien's bags Jordan didn't want him to know that someone had been going through them, so she was very careful. As she was going through the first bag, she saw that it was full of clothes and nothing else. So, she carefully put everything back and fastened up the bag. She saw that the next bag was full of food. Jordan didn't go through the other two bags because she assumed that they would be filled with much the same kind of things. But she was sure that they belonged to O'Brien. At this point, Jordan decided to give Lucas a call.

"Hello," said Lucas.

"Hi Lucas, it's Jordan. I think that I've found O'Brien's hideout."

"That sounds great, where?"

"Scrap yard in St Ives. You sound a little glum, what's the matter?" said Jordan.

"I'm at a scene of another murder. It looks like O'Brien's work," said Lucas.

"Where?" said Jordan.

"We're at your bed and breakfast," said Lucas.

"Who is it?" said Jordan.

"Hazel Davies, the owner," said Lucas.

"Okay, we'll be right there!" said Jordan.

At that, Jordan hung up and put her phone back in her jacket pocket. She then proceeded to tell Jarvis what had happened. At that, they went back to the car and made their way back to the bed and breakfast.

Jordan drove as quickly as she could to get back to the bed and breakfast. On the phone Jordan had only got some of the details from Lucas. Now, she wanted to see for herself exactly what had happened.

As she drove back to the bed and breakfast every set of traffic-lights seemed to be against her. But eventually they were approaching the building and Jordan could see a couple of police cars outside. As she got closer, she saw the CSI van pull up. Jordan couldn't find a parking spot outside the building so she had to go down the road a little bit. As she passed, she saw Lucas standing outside. When the car was parked they made their way back to the bed and breakfast. When they were close to the building, they saw that Lucas was still standing outside and they went straight up to him.

"What happened?" said Jordan.

"We don't know much just yet," said Lucas.

"What do you know?" said Jordan.

"One of the guests at the bed and breakfast arrived back earlier after spending some time at the beach. When she was making her way inside, she saw someone arguing with Hazel at the reception desk but carried on upstairs to her room. When she came back down about twenty minutes later to get some clean towels, she couldn't see her at reception. So, she went looking for her in the dining room. As she walked into the dining room that was when she found Hazel laying on the floor dead. I showed her a photo of O'Brien, she said that she thought that he could be the guy arguing with Hazel but she wasn't sure," said Lucas.

"Does she know what they were arguing about?" said Jordan.

"She doesn't know what the argument was about but she did hear a name being mentioned."

"Did she say who's?" said Jordan.

"Yeah, yours. It appears that he came here looking for you and you weren't here," said Lucas.

This information has changed the entire investigation. Jordan may no longer be a police officer but she was still part of the investigating team. There is now more urgency than ever to find and catch O'Brien. But as Jarvis and Lucas started to worry about Jordan's safety, Jordan saw this as an opportunity.

"I have an idea," said Jordan with a smile.

"What kind of idea?" said Jarvis with concern.

"To set a trap for O'Brien using me as bait."

"No, I don't like that idea," said Jarvis.

"Actually, it could do the trick. To make sure that no one overhears us let's go up to your room," said Lucas.

As the three of them went to Jordan's room to discuss Jordan's plan, Carl Benson, Jarvis's friend who'd asked Jordan to get involved with the case, was taking his dog for a walk. Carl was at the local park with his dog and he was wondering how the case was coming along. Carl always watched the news on TV but he knew that the news never reported all the information, so he made up his mind that he would give Jarvis a call when he arrived home.

Carl's dog was a little Jack Russell called Mac. Mac was off the lead at the moment and he was having a good wander around the park, but he was never too far away from Carl. It was a quiet day in the park with Carl being the only dog walker there. A little way in the distance Carl spotted someone walking in his general direction. At first,

Carl didn't pay them much attention, but that was about to change. As the person came a little closer Carl gave them another glance. It was at that point he thought that he recognised the person. When the person walked past him Carl was certain that he knew who the person was, that it was O'Brien, the killer.

Carl knew that he had to get hold of Jordan to tell her that he had just seen O'Brien. He called Mac over to him, put him on his lead then pulled out his mobile to give Jordan a call. Jordan was still in her room with Jarvis and Lucas when her mobile started to ring.

"Hello," said Jordan.

"Hello Jordan, it's Carl."

"Hi Carl, how are you?"

"I'm not too good to be honest, I've just seen O'Brien."

"Where?" said Jordan.

Carl went on to tell Jordan exactly where he was when he saw O'Brien. When he told her that he was still there but he was safe because O'Brien had carried on walking away from him, Jordan told him to stay put and that she would soon be there.

After the call, Jordan quickly updated Jarvis and Lucas. All three of them made their way down to their cars, then drove to where Carl was waiting for them. The three of them knew that this could be a perfect time to catch O'Brien.

Carl could just about see them from where he was standing and made his way over to them. He told them which direction O'Brien was heading. While Jarvis stayed with Carl, Jordan and Lucas went to see if they could find O'Brien. Luckily, they arrived at Carl's location within ten minutes of his phone call, so there a good chance that O'Brien was somewhere nearby.

At this point, O'Brien was still in the park but had found himself a hiding place. He knew that people were looking for him but he wanted time to think before he went back to the scrap yard. There was a small group of bushes where O'Brien was hiding and he was sat on the ground so no one could see him. As he sat there, he suddenly heard voices. As he listened to the voices, he thought that he recognised them. When the voices had gone by his hiding place and were far enough away O'Brien stood up to see who it was and he recognised Jordan and Lucas.

"Someone told them that you were here, they're looking for you!" said the voice.

Out of curiosity O'Brien wanted to know what they were up to, so he started to follow them. O'Brien had a real good look around to make sure that no one had noticed him, and he made sure that he kept a good distance from them because he didn't want to catch their attention.

"This is a very bad idea!" said the voice.

But as usual O'Brien ignored it. Both Jordan and Lucas could see that the park was quite large with plenty of potential hiding places. So, the two of them split up to have a look around. O'Brien was more interested in Jordan, so he followed her.

O'Brien was finding it difficult to stay out of Jordan's line of sight, however, as she was searching every potential hiding place on the off chance that O'Brien was hiding in one of them, little did she know that O'Brien was actually following her. The further they got from Lucas, the closer O'Brien got to Jordan.

While this was going on Lucas was searching his section of the park, totally unaware that Jordan was in potential danger. When Lucas had searched a large portion of his section of the park, he began to wonder how Jordan was coming along, so he gave her a call. But Lucas quickly became concerned about her as her phone rang out. After a short while he stopped calling Jordan and he gave Jarvis a call instead.

"Hello," said Jarvis.

"Hi Jarvis, it's Lucas. Is Jordan with you?"

"No, she isn't. Is there anything wrong?"

"The two of us split up to search for O'Brien. I've just tried calling her and she isn't answering."

At that, the two of them became highly concerned for Jordan's safety. They began to wonder if O'Brien had got his hands on her.

CHAPTER EIGHTEEN

———

With Jordan being missing and potentially kidnapped by O'Brien, Lucas wasn't going to take any chances. He called the station, told them the situation and asked for as many officers as possible to assist him in the search for Jordan. Then, he turned to Jarvis and suggested that he took Carl home, which he did.

Jarvis had a spare set of keys for Jordan's car so it wouldn't be a problem taking Carl home. When they were in the car, they made the journey to Carl's home in silence, as they were both so worried about Jordan.

When they were about a couple of minutes into the journey to Carl's house Jarvis spotted someone. He thought it might be Jordan, but he was past the person before he could have a good enough look. So the first opportunity he got, Jarvis pulled over.

"What are you doing?" said Carl.

"I think I've just seen Jordan," said Jarvis.

When the car was parked Jarvis got out and went back to the place, while Carl stayed with the car. Jarvis had a good look around and at first, he couldn't see anyone who resembled the person he'd just seen. But when he looked across the road, he swore he saw Jordan rushing up a side street.

The first chance he got Jarvis made his way across the busy main road and up the side street he thought he'd seen Jordan go up. When he walked up the street, he couldn't see anyone, but he knew whoever he saw come onto the street couldn't have gone far. So, Jarvis carried on down the street looking for whoever it was, just hoping that it was Jordan.

As he was walking down the street someone smashed what sounded like a glass bottle and Jarvis nearly jumped out of his skin. After a moment's pause Jarvis carried on down the street. Jarvis didn't want whoever it was to get too far away from him, so he picked up his pace. But he didn't have to go much further because when he went round the next corner, he saw the person who he thought was Jordan and to his dismay it wasn't her, it was someone completely different. Jarvis then, with disappointment, made his way back to the car.

"Well, was it her?" said Carl.

"No, it wasn't."

As Jarvis took Carl home, the officers that Lucas requested finally arrived. Lucas asked some of the officers to drive around the area to see if they could find Jordan. He then asked those who remained to search the park and not to leave any stone unturned. While on the search in the park Lucas would every so often give Jordan's mobile a call, but it just rang and rang and Lucas could never get Jordan to answer.

As Lucas put his own mobile back in his jacket pocket one of the officers shouted out to him. As Lucas walked over to the officer who shouted for him, he saw four other officers with him.

"Have you found something, then?" said Lucas.

"Yeah, I've found a mobile phone," said the officer.

As he looked on the ground Lucas could see the mobile phone. In one of his jacket pockets he had a pair of latex gloves and an evidence bag for just such an occasion. When he had put on one of the gloves Lucas bent down and picked up the phone. As he looked through the phone, he could tell that it belonged to Jordan. He now knew why she wasn't answering it – because it was no longer with her. This also meant Jordan couldn't call out for help if O'Brien had his hands on her.

As the search for Jordan continued O'Brien was back at the scrap yard. His anxiety was now worse than ever. He was pacing up and down the centre of the office.

"You really have done it now," said the voice.

O'Brien really didn't know what to do now. He didn't know whether to stay hiding out at the scrap yard or to leave Cornwall completely. Just then, he heard a noise coming from outside. He went straight over to the office widow to check it out. As he approached the window O'Brien crouched right down. He did this because if there was someone outside, he didn't want to be seen. At first, O'Brien couldn't see anyone or anything. But then something moved quickly past the window. Whatever it was moved so quickly O'Brien couldn't tell if it was someone or something.

"You need to get out of Cornwall, you need to get out now!" said the voice.

For a moment O'Brien didn't know what to do. What he did do was to stay crouched down and continue to look out of the window. Before he did anything, O'Brien wanted to know if there was a person in the yard or not. For the next few minutes, he just stared out of the office window in the hope that he caught sight of something. But after a few minutes of seeing nothing he decided to go outside for a look.

"This is a very bad idea," said the voice.

But O'Brien went outside anyway. At first, he opened the office door and just peered out. When he didn't see anything he eventually went out of the office. When he was just outside the office, he had a real good look around. As he did so he thought he saw something move near one of the scrap cars, so he went over for a closer look. As he walked over to the scrap car, he had a good look around the yard, but he didn't see anyone. When he reached the car, he walked all the way around it, but he still didn't see anyone or anything.

"See, just a figment of your imagination," said the voice.

Just then, O'Brien was pushed to the ground. He felt someone on top of him tying his wrists together. As he lay there on his stomach, he looked over his shoulder to see who was on top of him. As he did so he saw that it was Jordan who was on top of him tying his wrists together with some old rope that she had found in the yard.

As she tied his wrists together, she looked him in the eye and said: "I've got you."

When she had finished tying his wrists together Jordan went to get her mobile phone out of her jacket pocket, realising as she did so that she had lost her phone. Now, she had a dilemma: she had to get hold of Lucas but she didn't have her phone. She then remembered when she was here earlier with Jarvis there was a public payphone quite near the entrance gates. Jordan had another piece of rope so she sat O'Brien up and tied him to the scrap car. When she had done that, she went to the payphone to call Lucas. O'Brien wasn't happy at being tied up – Jordan left him cursing under his breath.

Jordan made her way to the phone box as quickly as she could. As she did so she thought about what had happened in the park earlier. While she was searching for O'Brien and he was following her, a few young kids came running past them shouting and screaming. This spooked O'Brien, so he made way out of the area as quickly as he could. Jordan noticed this and she started to follow him. As she did so her mobile phone fell out of her jacket pocket. By now Jordan had reached the phone box, so she called Lucas.

"Hello," said Lucas.

"Hey Lucas, it's Jordan."

"Where the hell are you? I have officers searching for you. We thought O'Brien had got his hands on you."

"I don't think so, I have him."

"What do you mean, you have him?"

"I've caught him, I have him tied up in the scrap yard in St Ives."

"Okay, I'm on my way with some officers. I've found your mobile phone by the way."

"Oh great, can you bring it with you please," said Jordan.

At that, the two of them hung up with Jordan making her way back to the scrap yard. When she arrived back O'Brien was still tied up where she had left him. Jordan went over to O'Brien and crouched next to him.

"Well, the police are on their way. When they get here you will be going to prison," said Jordan.

O'Brien just sat there and said nothing.

At that, Jordan stood up and walked back to the yard's gates to wait for Lucas and his men. Within a few minutes she saw them coming down the road with Lucas leading the way. To Jordan, it looked like he had brought a small army with him. When they were at the scrap yard and were out of there cars they walked over to Jordan.

"Well, where is he?" said Lucas.

"Just over here," said Jordan.

"Here is your mobile phone," said Lucas.

At that point, they went into the scrap yard. When they arrived where O'Brien was tied up, he was untied, placed in handcuffs, placed into the back of a police car and taken down to the police station. Little did anyone realise, but Jordan and the police officers were about to get a surprise, an unwanted surprise.

Jordan decided to go back to the station with Lucas. This was because she wanted to at least observe the interview with O'Brien. On the way to the station, she gave Jarvis a call to let him know that she was safe and where she was going. By now, Jarvis was with Carl at his home. When the phone call between the two of them was over Jarvis went to the station to be with her. Carl had heard every word of the conversation, so out of curiosity Carl also decided to go with Jarvis.

Soon, Jordan, the police and O'Brien were arriving at the police station. They all entered the building at the rear, so the public couldn't see what was happening. Plus, going in the back way took everyone straight to the cell area. When everyone was inside with the back door closed and locked, a couple of officers took O'Brien to an empty cell, took off his handcuffs and locked him inside. Then, a solicitor was called for to sit in with O'Brien for his interview.

While everyone waited for the solicitor to turn up, Jordan, Lucas and some of the uniformed officers sat in the break room. Everyone was so relaxed, cracking jokes and really enjoying having the killer in custody. Before long, the solicitor had arrived and Lucas gave the solicitor some time to talk to O'Brien in one of the interview rooms.

After about ten minutes O'Brien's solicitor appeared at the door of the interview room. At that, Lucas along with another officer went to interview O'Brien. In some of the corners of the ceiling of the interview room were a couple of video cameras, so that the interview could be recorded. Jordan went into the room where the interview was being recorded to watch the interview on the monitor. When she walked into the room there was already an officer in there. The two of them smiled at each other then settled down to watch the interview. All the way through the interview O'Brien said 'no comment' to every question he was asked. Try as he might Lucas couldn't get O'Brien to say anything else. After a couple of hours Lucas decided to give it a rest for a little while. As Lucas and the other officer walked out of the room, O'Brien did then say something different.

"It isn't over, yet."

"What do you mean, it isn't over yet?" said Lucas.

"You'll see," said O'Brien.

For another hour Lucas tried to get more out of him but O'Brien just sat there with a smile on his face. When he had

had enough, Lucas stood up and walked out of the room. At that, Jordan left the room with the monitors. As she stood up, she looked at the monitor one last time. As she looked at the monitor O'Brien looked at one of the cameras and smiled, as if he was smiling at her. This sent a chill up and down her spine. Then, Jordan left the room to talk to Lucas.

As she went to find Lucas Jordan received a text message. When she read it, she saw that it was from Jarvis saying that he had been waiting in the reception for quite a while for her. She texted him back saying that she shouldn't be too long now. Then, she went to find Lucas and found him in the break room.

"Well, what do you think?" said Jordan.

"To what?" said Lucas.

"To his comment when you were leaving the room for the first time."

"I'm not sure. It could mean that he has a partner, what do you think?"

"That's what I'm thinking, he could have a partner," agreed Jordan.

"Yeah, but how are we going to find out if he has a partner or not? I don't think O'Brien will tell us anything."

"If he does have a partner it could be one of two people. David Crammer or the stranger," said Jordan.

"Who's the stranger?"

"There's this guy who I've seen around who's taken a real keen interest in my investigation. I managed to talk to him earlier but he refused to give me his name."

"So, we need to talk to them, then."

"Yes, we do. You know what Crammer looks like, so you go and find him while I look for the stranger."

At that, they went their separate ways. Lucas knew that there was a file in the station on David Crammer which was about his previous convictions. In the file there would be a mugshot photo of David. So, Lucas went to find the file in the records department. When he found it, he took a few photocopies of the photo. When he had enough copies, he gathered a few uniformed officers together, gave them each a copy of the photo and asked them to search for Crammer. Lucas joined the search as well.

As Lucas did that Jordan started her search for the stranger. Jordan began by going to the reception area where Jarvis and Carl were waiting for her. She briefly explained to them what was happening, before beginning the search for the stranger. But first she took Carl home.

While Jordan was taking Carl home, the stranger was walking on the beach near Jordan's bed and breakfast. With it being a warm, sunny afternoon there were a good number of people on the beach. The stranger didn't like it too much being among a large number of people, so he went to the end of the beach where it was less crowded. At the end of the beach that the stranger was walking towards, was a large boulder. All the local kids loved to play on it. When the stranger was only a few feet from the boulder he could see a pair of feet. It was as if someone was sunbathing. The stranger didn't want to disturb the person, so he stopped where he was. While he was stood there, he decided that he had had enough of walking on the beach and wanted to go home. So, he started to look for a way off the beach. As he looked around, he saw that the nearest exit from the beach was just on the other side of the boulder.

As he walked past the boulder towards the exit he did so rather quietly, so as not to disturb the person who he thought was sunbathing. As he walked past the person, he could see that it was a young lady. When he gave her a second glance, he could see that she had her eyes open and it appeared she was looking at him, so he said hello. But when he didn't get a response, he looked at her more closely. This time, he thought that there was something a little strange about her, but he couldn't explain what. So, he went over to her, knelt down next to her and gave her a gentle nudge.

"Are you okay?" he said.

As he did so he realised that she was stone cold which explained why he didn't get a reply. He now knew he had to call the police but he remembered that he had left his mobile phone at home on charge, so he had to find himself a public phone. Just then, it dawned on him that a public phone wasn't too far from where he was, so he raced over to it. Once he was there, he called the police, told them about the body and where it was. When he was asked for his name, he hung up the phone. He didn't give his name because he didn't want to be involved in the investigation. Immediately after the phone call Lucas was informed of the dead body. Once he was told he jumped into his car and raced round to the beach.

On his way to the location, he gave Jordan a call. He told her about the body being found and its location. She had just left Carl at his home, so she made her way there as quickly as she could. Jarvis had decided to stay with Carl for a while, so Jordan was making her way to the scene by herself. On the way Jordan was wondering if this was O'Brien's last kill before he was caught.

Soon, Jordan was arriving at the scene. When she had parked her car, she walked the short distance to where the body was lying. As she walked there Jordan could see that a crowd was beginning to gather. When she was at the actual scene, she could see that an area was roped off with crime scene tape with the body within the area. There were uniformed officers keeping the small crowd back, Mandy Fletcher, the pathologist, was kneeling over the body and then she noticed Lucas. When Lucas saw Jordan, he went over to her.

"Well, what do you know?" said Jordan.

"Not much to be honest," said Lucas.

"Any idea of how long the victim has been dead?"

"No, not yet. We'll have to wait until Mandy has done her examination," said Lucas.

"Any idea of who called it in?"

"We have no idea, that caller didn't leave their name."

As they were talking Mandy, the pathologist, had finished her on-scene examination and she stood up. She gave the body one last look, then asked her two assistants to take the body to the morgue. Mandy looked around for Lucas. When she spotted him, she walked over to where he was stood.

"Any idea on the time of death?" said Lucas.

"I would say within the last two to four hours," said Mandy.

"Are you sure?" said Jordan.

"Yes, I'm very sure."

Now, Jordan and Lucas knew that they had a problem. They knew that O'Brien had been in custody for at least six hours. With this new body being dead for a maximum of four hours it meant they needed to look for a different murderer.

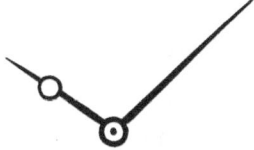

CHAPTER NINETEEN

——

While Jordan and Lucas were stood talking at the crime scene there was someone in the small crowd watching them. The stranger, the one who had found the body, had returned to the scene. He was interested to see whether Jordan would turn up. As the stranger was watching Jordan and Lucas, out of habit Jordan had a look round the small crowd that had gathered. From when she worked for the police, Jordan knew that sometimes the killer would return to the scene of the crime. So, she scanned the crowd to see if anyone stood out and she wasn't disappointed.

"That's interesting," said Jordan.

"What is?" said Lucas.

"The stranger that I mentioned at the station, well, he is stood over there in the crowd."

"Yeah, which one?" said Lucas.

"See the one in blue jeans and red jacket?"

"Yeah."

"That's him."

"How do you want to do this?"

"If you could have a couple of your officers go behind him, so if he tries to run, they can stop him. When they are in position we'll go and talk to him," suggested Jordan.

Lucas went to talk to a couple of officers. He asked them to do what Jordan had suggested. When they were in position Jordan and Lucas went to have a chat with the stranger. The stranger saw the two of them walking towards him. At that, he started to walk away, but the two officers stopped him.

"Where are you going in such a hurry?" said Jordan.

"As I've told you before, I don't want to be involved in your investigation," said the stranger.

"Then, what are you doing at a murder scene?" said Lucas.

"I have no comment to that."

"Well, I believe you have something to do with what happened here today," said Jordan.

"Well, I didn't. I only found the woman and called the police."

"You know, I think it would be better if we discuss this down the station," said Lucas.

As the stranger was being taken to the station Mark Barker, the journalist, had heard about the body being found. He had been at the scene for about fifteen minutes. As she was about to leave Jordan noticed him taking notes. Before she went to the station, to see what the stranger had to say for himself, she went to have a chat with Mark.

"I thought I would see you here," said Jordan.

"Yeah, a little birdie told me that there was something going on here," said Mark.

"I bet it did."

"So, this will be O'Brien's work, then?"

"Not this time, I'm afraid."

"What do you mean by that?"

"You'll find out in time."

At that, Jordan walked away. She went back to her car so that she could return to the station. Jordan wanted to know what the stranger had to say for himself. While she did that Mark wanted to know what she meant about O'Brien. Mark had a contact at the police station, so he gave him a call to see what he knew. When he managed to get hold of his contact Mark was told that O'Brien had been arrested and was in custody. This really got Mark thinking. Mark was wondering if O'Brien was in police custody then who had killed the latest victim? Now, Mark had something to investigate for himself. Mark wondered to himself whether David Crammer had anything do with the recent murder. Mark had last seen David earlier when he was following him. Now he had to find David again. So, he went back to the last place that he saw him, to do just that.

As Mark went to find David, Jordan, Lucas and the stranger were arriving back at the station. On the journey back to the station Jordan had an idea and she was really eager to tell Lucas about it. When they had arrived back, they went in the back way as they had done earlier, put the stranger into a cell and called for a solicitor to sit in with the stranger for his interview. As they waited for the solicitor to arrive, Jordan had a chat with Lucas.

"On the way back here, I came up with an idea," said Jordan.

"Yeah, and what's that?" said Lucas.

"Why don't we put these two in an interview room together while we watch them on a monitor. If they are working together, they may slip up and give us something."

"That might just work. I'll even give them a cup of tea each."

Lucas asked the officer on the reception desk to inform him when the solicitor for the stranger turned up. Then, they put Jordan's plan into motion. They took O'Brien out of his cell and put him in the interview room, then they did the same with the stranger. Jordan and Lucas watched the monitor to see if the plan would work. For several minutes the two of them just sat there in silence drinking their cups of tea. Then, O'Brien looked at the stranger.

"So, what have they dragged you in here for?" said O'Brien.

"They've brought me in here for the murder of a young woman. They think I may have something to do with this person they call the pocket watch killer," said the stranger.

"Really, tell me all about it," said O'Brien.

The stranger went on to tell O'Brien about the body he had found on the beach near Jordan's bed and breakfast. About how he had followed Jordan's investigation. And the stranger went into great detail as he told his story, but nothing incriminating was said the entire time. Before long the stranger's solicitor had arrived. At this point, O'Brien was put back in his cell with the stranger staying where he was.

When everyone was ready and in position the interview with the stranger began. As with the O'Brien's interview, this interview was conducted by Lucas with Jordan in the monitor room. All the way through the interview the stranger gave the exact same answers to every question that Lucas asked him. No answer was different from when Jordan and Lucas spoke to the stranger at the beach. After about an hour Lucas put a stop to the interview for the time being. As Lucas left the interview room Jordan made her way out of the monitor room. The two of them went to the far end of the corridor, away from the interview room, to have a chat.

"I think he's being truthful with us. I'll organise his release," said Lucas.

"Yeah, okay," said Jordan.

"You don't seem so sure, what's the matter?"

"I think he's being truthful, but I don't think he's telling us everything. You're able to keep hold of him for forty-eight hours without charge, so how about keeping hold of him, for now, to see what happens?"

"Okay, we'll do that, then."

While Jordan and Lucas continued with their investigation Mark was still looking for David Crammer. Mark returned to the area where he last saw David and worked outwards from there. After almost an hour of driving around with no sign of David, Mark was thinking about giving up for the day. With it getting late on in the afternoon Mark was thinking about going home. He didn't feel like cooking anything for his evening meal when he arrived home, but there was a fish and chip shop near his home, so, he went there for something to eat.

When he arrived at the fish and chip shop and had parked his car, Mark had to decide what he wanted to eat. When he walked into the shop and smelled all the food cooking, Mark suddenly became very hungry. When it was his turn to order Mark decided to be boring and he ordered fish and chips. When he had paid for his food and received his order, he made his way back to his car.

Back at his car and sat in the driver's seat, he heard a voice come from the back seat. When he looked in his rear-view mirror, he saw David Crammer sat there.

"You really need to learn to lock your car," said David.

"What do you want?" said Mark.

"To talk. But not here, let's go to your house."

At that, Mark put his fish and chips on the passenger seat, put on his seat belt, started his car and started to drive. Mark knew that he had to tell Jordan and the police about what was happening. But he didn't know, at this time, how or when he would be able to do that. Mark didn't really want David at his house, but he knew if he tried to take David to the police station or anywhere else, he would probably regret it. So, he drove to his house.

On the drive over Mark was wondering what David was planning. Then, Mark's professional mind came into play, and he started to think about his story for the newspaper. He was thinking if David had anything to do with these murders and he got some kind of confession, it would work wonders for his story.

Soon, they were arriving at Mark's house. When the car was parked, Mark grabbed his fish and chips, then the two of them got out of the car and made their way into Mark's house. When inside and he had taken off his coat, Mark offered David a cup of tea, which he accepted. Mark even shared his fish and chips with David. Once they were sat at the dining table the two of them started to talk.

"So, why do you want to talk to me?" said Mark.

"I want to talk to you about these murders," said David.

"Yeah, what about these murders, then?"

"Let's just say that everything isn't as it seems."

"And what do you mean by that?" said Mark.

"What I am saying is that Mike O'Brien isn't the only one involved."

For the next couple of hours, the conversation followed the same theme. To Mark, David was admitting his involvement in the murders without actually saying it. At this point, Mark made the excuse that that he wanted to go to the toilet. On the way to the bathroom Mark managed to grab his mobile phone without David seeing him. While in the bathroom Mark managed to give Jordan a call. Mark had to whisper. He told her about David Crammer being at his house and why he was there. Mark told her the address and finished the call. Luckily, Jordan was still at the police station. She told Lucas what was going on and he got some officers together and they all made their way to Mark's house.

While Jordan and the police were making their way to Mark's house, Mark went back downstairs to talk to David. As he was about to leave the bathroom Mark heard something just outside on the other side of the door. As he stood at the door listening Mark suddenly heard a voice.

"Hey Mark, have you nearly finished? Because I could do with using the toilet," said David.

"I won't be a minute," said Mark.

Mark made sure his mobile phone was in his pocket. Then, he flushed the toilet to make David think that he had just used it, then he came out of the bathroom. As David went in Mark came downstairs. Mark had a look out of the front room window to see if Jordan and the police had arrived, but there was no sign of them. Mark heard the toilet being flushed, then he heard David coming out of the bathroom. At that, Mark went and sat down, but he sat down in a chair so that he could keep a look out for Jordan and the police. As soon as he sat down, he saw David coming downstairs. David sat in the armchair opposite Mark.

"So, what else do you know about these murders?" said Mark.

"I can tell you more than you could ever imagine," said David.

"What I'm curious about is how do you know what you know about these murders. Are you involved somehow?"

"What do you think?"

But before Mark could answer some cars could be heard pulling up outside. David immediately stood up and looked out of the window. He could see the police had come in numbers, but the person he saw practically straight away was Jordan. Then, he looked directly at Mark.

"You called the police on me?"

At that, Crammer went running out of the back door. At the same time Mark went to the front door.

"He's gone running out of the back door," said Mark.

Jordan came running through the house to go the same way as David, with Lucas and his men going round the back. Jordan went through the back door into the back yard. She saw that the gate to the yard was open and she went through it. When she was through the gate Jordan found herself in an alley. With her not knowing exactly where David was, she slowed down. As she walked down the alley, she looked for any movement as well as listening for any noises, but she didn't see or hear anything. Just then, Lucas appeared at the end of the alley.

"Where is he?" said Lucas.

"I don't know but he couldn't have gone far," said Jordan.

At that, Jordan, Lucas and the other officers went from street to street in search for David Crammer. They knew that David could be the last piece of the jigsaw in solving the case. What they didn't know was that Jordan was actually right, David wasn't too far away. He was hiding in one of the other back yards down the alley behind Mark's house.

David gave it a few minutes for Jordan and the police to move away from the alley. When he couldn't hear them anymore, David came out of the back yard to try and get out of the area. When he was at the end of the alley David peered out to make sure that no one was there to see him. When he was happy that no one was there, David made his way out of the alley and out of the area.

Now that it was early evening the sun was beginning to go down with the daylight beginning to fade. By now Jordan, Lucas and the other officers had covered a fair bit of ground. They were at the point where they were thinking that David had got away. Then, on an officer's radio, an officer who was near Jordan and Lucas, a call was going out that David had been seen, with the location. Jordan, Lucas and the other officers raced back to Mark's house as quickly as they could, got into their cars and drove to the area where David had been spotted as quickly as they could.

When they had arrived in the right place, they could see that it was a wooded area with trees and bushes. When they were out of their cars Jordan and Lucas were told that the person thought to be David had been seen going into the trees. So, Lucas told everyone to search the trees. With the daylight becoming more gloomy torches would have to be used for the search. Jordan didn't have a torch but Lucas had a spare, so he loaned her one.

When everyone was basically in one line and ready, the search of the trees began. The search team looked behind every tree, every bush and every possible hiding place. The person who was thought to be David could see the police searching, but they continued their journey through the trees. The person that was ahead of the police twisted their ankle quite badly. After a moment's pause, they continued on their journey through the trees, but the twisted ankle had slowed them down. But soon an officer in the search spotted the person ahead of them. The officer called out to them to stop, but they didn't. With the officer calling out, Jordan, Lucas and the rest of the search party spotted the person ahead of them. With the off chance of it being David they all picked up their pace to catch up with the person.

With the person ahead of them twisting his ankle the search party were beginning catch up with him. They were getting closer and closer to him. When they were almost within touching distance of the person, everyone suddenly lost sight of him. It was as if he had disappeared into thin air.

"Where did he go?" said Jordan.

"I don't know, it's as if he's just vanished," said Lucas.

"He has to be here. We all need to concentrate our search to this immediate area," said Jordan.

At that, every tree, every bush and every blade of grass was searched. When nothing was found the immediate area was searched again. After about forty-five minutes nobody could find the person that they had been chasing. Then, for a moment Jordan and Lucas just looked at each other in disbelief. Nobody liked it but they all had to concede defeat. Now, the search party started to leave the area. Jordan was the last to leave and she gave the area one last look before she left. As she turned to leave with everyone else, Jordan heard something. To Jordan it sounded like a sneeze, but as if someone had tried to sneeze quietly. The noise she heard seemed quite close to her, so she had another look. As she did so Lucas noticed her still searching, so he went over to her.

"Is everything okay?" said Lucas.

"There's someone just here," said Jordan.

Lucas called over a couple of officers to assist them search this particular area. After a minute or so of searching they heard some movement. Just then, someone stood up just in front of Jordan. Straight away they could see that it was David Crammer.

"Stay right there, don't move," said Lucas.

One of the uniformed officers placed David in handcuffs. Then, they took David to one of the police cars. When he was placed in one of the cars, they took him to the station for questioning. Once at the station Jordan called Jarvis and told him what was happening.

Epilogue

With it being late in the evening it was decided to leave David Crammer's interview until the following morning. Before they left the station for the night, Jordan and Lucas had a chat about the stranger. The two of them came to an agreement that he didn't have anything to do with the murders. So, for the last job of the day, Lucas supervised the stranger's release. Jordan, out of curiosity, had one question for the stranger. So, she went along with Lucas. The stranger was taken from the cell to the main desk in the holding area. While the desk sergeant dealt with the paperwork Jordan, Lucas and the stranger had a chat.

"Now that you've been cleared of any wrongdoing, out of curiosity, what's your name?" said Jordan.

"Jake Mills."

"Why, Jake, have you been so interested in my investigation?" said Jordan.

"I was interested in the case from the start, but when you came into the case you added a little twist to it," said Jake.

"Well, in future try not to get so involved with things," said Jordan.

At that, Jake was taken to the front of the station and released. Then, within a couple of minutes of Jake leaving Jordan was making her way to her car. When she was in her car, she made her way to Carl's house to pick up Jarvis. While she was at Carl's, he paid her for the work she had done. Then, he made her a cup of coffee. As she drank her coffee the three of them had a chat.

"So, you caught the bad guy, then?" said Carl.

"Yes, we did. But actually, it looks like there were two of them," said Jordan.

"Two?" said Carl.

"Yeah, as well as Mike O'Brien it looks like David Crammer was also involved," said Jordan.

"It only looks like Crammer was involved, then?" said Jarvis.

"I would say that he was definitely involved, but all the facts will be cleared up tomorrow when Lucas interviews Crammer," said Jordan.

They talked for a little while longer while Jordan finished her coffee. Then, Jordan and Jarvis made their way back to the bed and breakfast for a well-earned sleep. Carl walked the two of them to the car. Just before she drove off Carl thanked Jordan again for all her hard work.

When they were back in their rooms at the bed and breakfast the two of them packed their bags so they would be ready to leave in the morning. When she had finished packing, Jordan wasn't quite ready to go to sleep just yet. So, she just lay on top of the bed thinking. She began to think about the case in general. In the main, she was really pleased with how the case had gone, especially the end result. But she had this nagging feeling that it wasn't quite finished. Eventually tiredness overcame her, so, she went to bed and she was soon falling asleep.

Before they knew it, it was the following morning. With Hazel, the bed and breakfast owner, being murdered they weren't sure if there would be any breakfast this morning. So, they went down to check. When they were downstairs, they saw the other guests were having their breakfasts, so they went into the dining room for theirs. Jordan and Jarvis knew that they had a long journey home, so they ate their breakfast as quickly as they could. When they had finished eating Lucas came walking into the dining room and joined them.

"Sorry, but we've eaten everything," Jordan said with a smile.

"That's okay, I've already eaten," said Lucas.

"Have you interviewed David Crammer yet?" said Jordan.

"Not yet, I'll be doing that later, I wanted to catch you before you left. I wanted to thank you for all the hard work that you've done on this case. And to say that the next time you're in Cornwall the drinks will be on me," said Lucas.

"I aim to collect," said Jordan with a smile.

"Excuse me, Miss Lewis, but this was left at reception for you," said a young lady.

"Thank you. Could you get our bill ready please, because we are leaving this morning," said Jordan.

"Okay."

Then, Jordan's attention went on to the envelope she had just been given. When she opened it and pulled out its contents, she saw that it was a pocket watch with a sympathy card. On the sympathy card the message said, "In Loving Memory of Hazel". For a moment or so the three of them just sat there and looked at each other, stunned. Then, the young lady came back to the table with Jordan's bill.

"Excuse me, but when was this handed in at the reception desk?" said Jordan.

"It was on the reception desk when Hazel was found dead," she said.

"O'Brien must have left it," said Lucas.

Jordan gave the items to Lucas as evidence. Then, Jordan's mobile phone started to ring. When she answered it she heard a voice.

"At the next tone it will be eight o'clock precisely," said the voice.

When Jordan heard the talking clock, she knew that she had to go home and go home quickly.

THE END